Cornelia
and the Audacious Escapades of the Somerset Sisters

For Caitlin, Franny, and Gregory

This is a work of fiction. Names, characters, places, and incidents either
are the product of the author's imagination or are used fictitiously. Any resemblance
to actual persons, living or dead, events, or locales is entirely coincidental.

ISBN-13: 978-0-545-05732-5
ISBN-10: 0-545-05732-9

Copyright © 2006 by Lesley M. M. Blume.
All rights reserved. Published by Scholastic Inc., 557 Broadway, New York, NY 10012,
by arrangement with Alfred A. Knopf, an imprint of Random House
Children's Books, a division of Random House, Inc. SCHOLASTIC and
associated logos are trademarks and/or registered trademarks of Scholastic Inc.
Lexile is a registered trademark of MetaMetrics, Inc.

12 11 10 9 8 7 6 5 4 3 2 1   8 9 10 11 12 13/0

Printed in the U.S.A.   40

First Scholastic printing, March 2008

Cornelia and the Audacious Escapades of the Somerset Sisters

Lesley M. M. Blume

SCHOLASTIC INC.
New York Toronto London Auckland Sydney
Mexico City New Delhi Hong Kong Buenos Aires

Chapter One

Cornelia

It was winter in New York City and the days were short.
At three o'clock in the afternoon, the sun already hung
low over the horizon, casting sharp pink light on the
clouds above the skyscrapers.

Cornelia S. Englehart lagged five steps behind her
classmate Lauren Brannigan as they walked down the
street. School had just ended for the day.

Lauren wheeled around to face Cornelia, her long
blond braids whipping through the air. "Come *on*, Cornelia," she said irritably, as if Cornelia were her annoying little sister. "Hurry up."

Cornelia reluctantly quickened her pace.

"So, what do you want to do this afternoon?" Lauren

asked without enthusiasm after they had walked several blocks in complete silence.

Now, in certain circles, Cornelia was renowned for her extreme reserve. Some girls always have a coterie of pretty friends, sisters, and cousins fluttering around them—but not her. She spent most of her time alone and hadn't had playmates since nursery school. Party invitations and after-school playdates had become few and far between. And when Cornelia *did* get asked over to someone's house, she was terribly out of practice and awkward.

"We can do whatever you want," Cornelia answered, her breath forming a misty cloud in the cold air.

Lauren sighed impatiently. "Well, I just got some new American Girl play scripts for Christmas," she said. "Maybe we can dress up and act one of them out."

Cornelia's heart sank. "I've never done a play before," she said, longing for her warm bedroom at home, with her armchair and all of her books.

"Fine," Lauren said. "My older sister just got a karaoke machine as one of her presents. Why don't we use that?"

What a nightmare, Cornelia thought. "I don't like singing either," she said.

Lauren lost her patience. "What *do* you like to do, then?" she snapped, staring at Cornelia.

"We could play Scrabble," Cornelia suggested. It

would give her secret satisfaction to trounce Lauren in the game, for Cornelia knew lots of uncommon words. It was her special weapon.

"That is *so* boring," said Lauren as she strode down the street. "But better than nothing, I suppose."

They arrived at Lauren's brownstone house and rang the front doorbell. When they heard the sound of footsteps coming toward the door from inside, Lauren whispered to Cornelia, "The only reason I invited you over in the first place is because my mother made me."

She smiled meanly as Cornelia's face turned ashen. At that moment, Mrs. Brannigan yanked the front door open.

"Hello, girls," she cried, clapping her hands together in apparent joy. "Come in, come in. It's absolutely *freezing* out there! Hello, hello, Cornelia! Welcome to our humble home. It's about time you came over and visited us. Ever since I heard that you were in Lauren's class, I have been simply *begging* Lauren to invite you over to play. And you live *so* nearby as well." She took the girls' coats and stuffed them into the front closet. "Follow me, troops—I have a snack for you in the kitchen," she shouted as she practically galloped down the front hallway.

Lauren glared at her guest as she followed her mother to the kitchen. Cornelia trailed after them.

"Sit down, ladies, sit down," Mrs. Brannigan

whooped, clattering down some plates, cupcakes, and glasses of milk for the girls. Cornelia, who found Mrs. Brannigan as volatile as a pot of boiling water, warily sat down at the kitchen table. Mrs. Brannigan plunked down in the chair next to her.

Lauren stomped to the refrigerator. "I want Sprite, not milk," she complained. "I'm not five years old, in case you forgot." Of course, she didn't offer Cornelia any soda as she poured herself a huge glass.

Mrs. Brannigan gave a little hoot. "Have whatever you want, dearest, as long as it's not brandy," she said, and smiled coyly at her cleverness. Then she swiveled around and leaned in toward Cornelia as if they were long-lost friends.

"*So*, my dear," Mrs. Brannigan said. "How *is* that mother of yours?"

"Fine," Cornelia replied, wishing by now that she were at the bottom of the ocean. The cupcake sat like a wart on the plate in front of her.

"I heard her play in a concert at Carnegie Hall last month," Mrs. Brannigan said. "Marvelous, absolutely *marvelous*! She has such flair, and my goodness, is she gorgeous! Those long, elegant arms! I could just *die*! I imagine that you play the piano too, don't you?"

"No," said Cornelia.

"*What?*" shrieked Mrs. Brannigan. "You *don't*? How can that be? I would think that your parents would insist! Especially since you're their only child, and all of that talent would go to *waste* if you didn't play too! After all, your father is a famous pianist also, isn't he?"

Cornelia stared at her glass of milk. "Yes, he is," she said after a moment. "But I've never met him."

For the first time since the girls had walked through the front door, the room was utterly silent. Even Lauren stared at Cornelia.

Mrs. Brannigan shifted uncomfortably in her chair. "Ohhh," she said. "I see. Well, that's *all right,* dear." She patted Cornelia's hand in a fakey, consoling manner.

Then she went on, "In any case, your mother seems *so* fabulous. I have always wanted to get to know her! She seems very warm. And, you see, I am planning this charity gala—a big party—and I'm *sure* it would be a big hit if your mother played the piano at it."

Tears sprang to Cornelia's eyes. *Now* she understood the invitation to Lauren's house. Believe it or not, this sort of thing had happened to her before. It always astonished Cornelia that adults were willing to make such fools of themselves in front of her just to get the chance to meet her famous mother.

"I think I'll go home now," she said, feeling older than her eleven years. "I have a stomachache." She got up and began to walk toward the front door. Lauren looked elated for the first time that afternoon.

"Ohhhh," wailed Mrs. Brannigan, sensing that her

mission was in danger. "What's the matter, sweetie?" She followed Cornelia down the hallway and snatched an envelope from a desk in the foyer.

"Just a second, dear," she cried, handing the envelope to Cornelia. "Please give this to your mother. And come back anytime! I mean it—absolutely *any*time!"

Cornelia put on her coat, marched out the front door, and closed it behind her, sealing Mrs. Brannigan back up inside. Cornelia sighed with relief. Her visit had lasted a grand total of ten minutes, nearly a record high for an after-school social outing.

She looked at the letter in her hand. "To Lucy" was scrawled on the front of the envelope. "Please call me!" was written on the back of it.

Cornelia dropped it in the gutter and went for a stroll.

Cornelia loved walking around her city neighborhood, Greenwich Village. She had never lived anywhere else, and it had been a wonderful place to grow up. Usually when people thought of New York City, they conjured up images of steel buildings tall enough to touch the sky, and wide avenues filled with rumbling taxis and buses. They thought of noise and dirt and crowds.

But Greenwich Village was different, like a world within a world. Its narrow streets wound around in a wonderful maze, and worn-down cobblestones covered many of them instead of plain old asphalt. People in the Village did not live in towering skyscrapers. They lived in rows of colorful brick houses with pretty trees and flower beds out front. Dogs of every shape and size briskly walked their owners up and down the sidewalks. Sometimes Cornelia forgot that she lived in a big city at all. Greenwich Village felt like, well, a small village, the sort of place where parents let children play ball in parks by themselves.

Cornelia liked exploring alone. She knew every building, nook, and cranny in the area. She loved visiting the Magnolia Bakery on Bleecker Street. In the front window, the bakers arranged lines of dainty cupcakes covered with pale pink, baby blue, or buttery yellow frosting. Cornelia's mother called them "fairy cakes," and customers stood in long lines down the block just to buy one. When the line was too long, Cornelia sometimes went around the corner to a tiny café called Westville instead. She ordered French fries and a root beer and watched people outside rush past the window. She made up stories about the passersby that she never told to anyone else.

However, the Biography Bookshop on Bleecker Street was Cornelia's favorite destination. She always marched past the tilting stacks of books written for girls her age and headed straight for the dictionary section. There she inspected the books for new arrivals. After all, Cornelia had an impressive dictionary collection of her own, and she needed to stay up to date.

Sometimes, if she was in the mood, she visited Cornelia Street. Cornelia's mother, Lucy, had lived there when she'd first moved to New York City, long before Cornelia was born. And then, when Cornelia came along years later and they moved to a bigger apartment, Lucy gave her new baby the most unusual name: Cornelia Street Englehart. Lucy's grown-up friends thought this was just wonderful, but Cornelia did not. In public, she shortened her name to Cornelia S. Englehart and kept her full identity to herself.

Today, Cornelia just sat in a nearby park and tried to forget about Lauren and her mother. When the sun finally started setting at four o'clock, she walked to her home on Greenwich Street. The big brick building where she lived looked like a Roman fortress with its rounded corners and arched windows. The Hudson River ran past it, two short blocks away. Cornelia squeezed through the heavy front doors into the grand foyer.

"Miss Englehart," boomed a voice from the front desk. "Might I 'ave a moment of your time, please?"

Walter Withycombe, the building's sociable, plump old doorman, peered down at Cornelia. White hair stuck out in tufts on his head, from his nostrils and ears, and even on his fingers with their knobby joints.

His eyes always smiled and he talked to children with the same level of respect as he did to adults. He had grown up in London, and he loved to tease the building's tenants in his loud, cockney-accented voice. Cornelia was his favorite target, and he always enjoyed catching her as she tried to slip unnoticed into the elevator.

He disappeared into the big, dark closet behind the front desk and reemerged with a large, banged-up box. Tape and string wound around it like a mummy and stamps covered the top.

"Tell Madame Desjardins to leg it down 'ere straightaway and get this parcel," Walter said. "I rung 'er on the phone about it hours ago." He drummed his fingers on the top of the box as he talked. Madame Desjardins was Cornelia's French housekeeper.

"Where is it from? Who sent it?" Cornelia asked. She stood on her tiptoes to see the stamps.

Walter investigated the writing on the box. "It's from your mum," he announced. "Blimey—she's in Moscow? Where 'asn't that lady been?"

Cornelia ignored his questions. "I'll tell Madame Desjardins to come down and get it," she said.

"Tell 'er to get it tonight or I'll throw it away," Walter threatened jovially. "It'll go straight into the bin! I *mean* it this time," he called after Cornelia as she got into the elevator and the door slid shut.

Somber as a widow, Walter thought to himself, shaking his head. *I 'spect all she needs is a spot of sunshine. Miss Lucille should take 'er along on a trip once in a while.*

He dropped the box under the desk with a thud.

Madame Desjardins opened the front door of the apartment with great flourish and ushered Cornelia in.

"Where have you been, Cornelia Street?" she exclaimed as Cornelia wiggled out of her backpack straps. "I began to think that you were blown away in the wind! *Mon Dieu,* your cheeks are cold." She hung up Cornelia's coat.

Madame Desjardins had been working for Lucy since Cornelia was born. It had been a decade filled with constant talking. Even though the housekeeper's English was proficient at best, she managed to fill every second of the day with chatter, and she was as nosy as a detective. An old-fashioned servant, she wore a white apron even when she did errands.

"Walter says that there's a box for us downstairs," Cornelia said. "It's from my mother."

"A box?" Madame Desjardins answered distractedly, taking the book bag into the kitchen. Cornelia followed her. "Oh, *oui.* Yes. I forgot. I will send Ingrid down when she is done with the living room. I am scared to ask her, though, for today she is in a worse mood than ever."

Ingrid was their maid. She came twice a week to give the apartment a vicious cleaning.

"Would you like a cup of tea?" asked Madame Desjardins, whisking a teakettle off the stovetop and heading for the sink.

"No, thank you," said Cornelia. "I'm just going to go upstairs to read until dinner."

"*Comment?* What? But you have only just come home," said Madame Desjardins, the kettle hanging at her side. "You do not want to tell me about school or your visit with the Brannigan girl, *l'enfant terrible?* Maybe I will come upstairs to sit with you. I am lonely today, with no one but Ingrid to speak with. Your mother is always away and you are too quiet." She looked at Cornelia as pitifully as possible.

"I want to read," said Cornelia. She had to be firm, for privacy was as rare as diamonds in a household run by Madame Desjardins. "But I'll come down when Ingrid gets the package," she added generously, and she ran out of the room.

Cornelia's home had an upstairs and a downstairs, which was unusual for an apartment in New York City. Extra-shiny wood covered the floors in all of the rooms and high ceilings loomed overhead. The apartment could easily be mistaken for a vast white museum instead of a house, for several enormous paintings hung on the walls and isolated clusters of modern furniture stood in the rooms. The dramatic spareness of the décor had a single purpose: to make the star of the house, Cornelia's mother, stand out as much as possible.

On the other hand, the apartment always made Cornelia herself seem smaller than she really was. Her footsteps echoed off the walls as she hustled down the corridor to the stairs.

Then she noticed that the big double doors to her mother's music room had been left open. Cornelia looked back toward the kitchen, but Madame Desjardins was clanging some pots around and showed no signs of emerging. Ingrid made some crashing noises down in the living room. Since no one was paying any attention, Cornelia ducked into the room where her mother spent her every waking moment when she was at home in New York.

The room's complicated beauty always intimidated Cornelia and made her feel out of place. It smelled slightly of old papers and cigarette smoke, and even more slightly of Chanel No. 5, an expensive perfume worn by Cornelia's mother. Dark, opulent wine-red silk covered the walls, and huge white bookshelves towered to the ceiling on two sides of the room. Hundreds of music books, written on coarse yellow and tan pages, lined the shelves. Every page in every book featured an intricate web of lines and notes, which only Lucy could read.

In the middle of the room stood a huge, sleek grand piano. It looked as important as a king on a chessboard, and its black lacquer gleamed like a mirror. Its row of shining black and white keys looked like a wide, teeth-baring grin. Madame Desjardins called the instrument the *"Bête Noire,"* which meant "black beast," and she never went near it.

The only person who ever touched the *Bête Noire* was Cornelia's mother, who was indeed a very famous concert pianist. And she was the only person in the apartment who understood the instrument at all. In fact, she loved it, seemingly more than anything else in the world. In return, the piano seemed to love Lucy with all of its heart, which was made of wire and felt and wooden hammers beating and moving and twanging in-side its massive body. To everyone else, the piano was indifferent and haughty.

When Cornelia was a very little girl, she used to loll under the piano while her mother practiced. She would lie on her stomach and watch Lucy's feet working the pedals as the music thundered from the *Bête Noire*'s belly above her. But as she got older, Cornelia grew wary of the instrument, and considered it her foremost enemy in the battle for Lucy's attention.

Cornelia poked around the room for a few minutes, breathing in its musty scent. Ingrid had straightened up, pushing stacks of music books usually strewn about on the floor into neat piles. Being inside the room made Cornelia miss her mother, who was at this very moment performing in a concert far away, halfway around the globe. Cornelia disliked her home when her mother was gone. The rooms in the apartment came alive only when Lucy was here and music was coming from the very room in which Cornelia stood.

She walked over to a large window and peered outside at the Hudson River. It looked cold and fierce, and loneliness trickled down inside her. After a few minutes, she went upstairs to her room and closed the door.

Outside, evening deepened into night and Cornelia's room darkened. She sat in her armchair, thumbing through a book and enjoying the relative quiet of her space. Like the music room downstairs, Cornelia's bedroom had tall bookshelves in it, most of which were crammed with books. Toys and stuffed animals that she had outgrown lined the hard-to-reach top shelves.

Cornelia's favorite shelf contained her precious dictionaries. Some of them were leather-bound; others were clad in tattered, faded canvas covers. She even had a thesaurus that had been owned by a famous writer who'd lived in Cuba and Spain and France, and had written about wars and bullfighting. It had been a present from Lucy, who was amused by her daughter's precocious interest in words.

While Cornelia loved reading books, her interest in dictionaries and complicated words had more to do with warding off people who tried to strike up lengthy conversations with her. Her life was simply too full of grown-ups who always looked over her shoulder or pestered her or peppered her with annoying questions about her family. Long, confusing words were often her only defense against the artillery of adults who plagued her.

The primary offender was Madame Desjardins, who, as it has been noted, still stuck to the simpler expressions of English as though she were clinging to the wall of an ice-skating rink. Whenever Madame Desjardins became too pesky or intrusive, Cornelia simply filled her sentences with longer and longer and increasingly inscrutable words. Finally, Madame Desjardins would bluster her speech to a halt and stare at Cornelia in a frustrated sort of way with her hands on her hips. "*Mon Dieu!* You are too much," she would say, and stomp down the hallway.

This afternoon, Cornelia's book of choice was *The Superior Person's Book of Words.* The inside flap of the book advertised the following: "Put an end to fopdoodly speech; amaze your friends, baffle your enemies, write interoffice memos to end all discussion!" Cornelia had neither friends nor enemies, and she did not even know what an interoffice memo was, but the idea of ending all discussion sounded good to her.

She soon had a chance to see if the book worked. She heard the telltale *thump, thump, thump* of Madame Desjardins's footsteps as she heaved up the stairs and knocked on Cornelia's door.

"Cornelia Street! May I please enter?" wheezed Madame Desjardins. She was quite portly, and the trip up the stairs always drained her. Without waiting for Cornelia's answer, she pushed the door open.

"Why are you reading with no light on?" she exclaimed as she clumped into the room. She descended upon an unsuspecting desk lamp and clicked it on. "You will ruin your eyes. And then you will have to wear big glasses and then none of the boys will want to kiss you when you grow up!" she practically shouted.

Cornelia just sat there, dumbfounded by this grander-than-usual entrance. "Madame Desjardins, I'm trying to read," she said.

"What is that little book?" Madame Desjardins swooped in and nudged the book backward so she could see the title. "Eeeee! Another book of words," she cried in despair, knowing a foe when she saw one. "Why do you not read books like the other girls want to read?

Like, let me think—like *Harriet ze Spy* or any of those Harry Potter books?"

Cornelia glanced down at page 68 of the book and found help right away. "Madame Desjardins, could you end this nugatory line of questioning and tell me what you want?" she asked, just warming up. "Nugatory" reportedly meant "pointless" or "trifling."

Her arrow met its target. *"Comment?"* squawked Madame Desjardins. "I want only to know what you would like to eat this evening. And what did you just say to me, young lady?" she added suspiciously.

Cornelia casually flipped to pages 84 and 85 and found a treasure trove of relevant words. "Please don't be a quidnunc, Madame Desjardins," she replied. "Must this conversation be quotidian? I find that quisquous."

She said this last word without even knowing if she pronounced it correctly. The word "quidnunc" meant "one who is forever anxious to know about everything that is going on." "Quotidian" meant "occurring every day," while "quisquous" meant "puzzling."

"Whatever you provide for sustenance will suffice," she finished. This meant that Madame Desjardins could cook anything she wanted. Cornelia sat back to watch the reaction to her speech unfold.

"Eeeeeeeeeeeiiiiiieeeeeeeeeeeee!!!" Madame Desjardins shrieked. "Every day you do this! I will be like a

crazy woman when I leave this house someday. *Mon Dieu!*"

"You are being a virago, Madame Desjardins!" Cornelia pressed on, growing a little excited that things were going so well. "Virago" meant "a fierce, bad-tempered woman," according to page 111.

"Fine! I will make spaghetti with meat, and you will just have to be happy with it." She flounced out of the room and closed the door.

A little later, once the storm clouds had cleared and the smell of tomato sauce wafted up the stairs, Madame Desjardins shouted from the kitchen, "Mademoiselle Dictionnaire! Come down the stairs. We will open the box." Cornelia threw her new favorite book on her bed and ran down the stairs.

Ingrid grouchily lugged the box into the living room. It looked like it might have suffered a few petulant kicks in the elevator on the way up. She dropped the box with an "Ouff!" and turned to Madame Desjardins, who stood there with a pair of scissors, waiting to cut the package open.

"Maid," Ingrid grunted, pointing to her own chest. "I'm a *maid,* not a manual laborer. That might mean the same thing in France, Madame Overseer, but in America, that's two different categories." She gathered her coat and bag. "See you on Saturday. If my back isn't broken," she muttered, looking darkly at the box.

Madame Desjardins dismissed her with a wave of her hand and zealously cut the tape and strings off the box. "This time, there will be a present for you, I can feel it," she said to Cornelia, sawing and snipping away.

A surge of hope swelled up in Cornelia, followed immediately by a thump of doubt. Did Lucy really think about her daughter while she was away? Did she even think about Cornelia while she was *here*, for that matter? Cornelia looked at the package with a new urgency, as if its opening might answer these questions. Her stomach tightened.

The box finally groaned and gave in, and Madame Desjardins tore open the top. She started pulling things out of it. "Let me see—some clothes . . . and, umm . . . programs from her concert! You can see where your mother is playing. And . . . umm . . . music books— I think she has played Chopin this time."

Madame Desjardins's stacks of clothes, books, and paper next to the box grew higher and higher.

"Aha!" she exclaimed, fishing a shoe box out of the bottom of the parcel. "I bet this is a little present for Mademoiselle Dictionnaire," she said, nodding at Cornelia.

"You open it," Cornelia said dubiously.

Madame Desjardins cut off some Scotch tape on the sides of the shoe box and took the top off.

"Oh," she said quietly, and her face changed. She

looked up at Cornelia. "Not this time after all. *Quel dommage*. What a pity. Maybe she is bringing the present when she comes home this weekend."

She reached into the shoe box and pulled out a pair of glamorous satin evening shoes with very tall heels. The strap on one of them was broken. Lucy had scrawled some words on the lid of the shoe box: "Please have fixed ASAP!"

Cornelia tried to swallow back her misery, determined not to cry in front of the housekeeper, but Madame Desjardins cooed and petted her sympathetically anyway. That evening, she made Cornelia a chocolate tart to eat while she did her homework.

The dejection still sat on Cornelia's chest like a rock when she was tucked into bed that night. She lay in the dark of her room, listening to the faint sounds of Madame Desjardins laughing at something on the television in her room down the hall, and then she began to cry. It had been a bad day and tomorrow would be more of the same. She'd wake up, go to school, sit alone at lunch, and now she would have to avoid even looking in Lauren Brannigan's direction on top of everything else. And then, after school, Cornelia would walk home slowly and spend the afternoon and evening enduring the excessive fussing of Madame Desjardins. Even when her mother came home again this weekend, it would only be a matter of days or weeks before Lucy would leave yet again for another concert in another city or country.

The cold January wind squeezed in around the edges of the bedroom window, slightly blowing the shades. Cornelia made a bet with herself that no other girl in her class felt as lonely as she did.

Chapter Two

Lucy

A week passed, and as Cornelia had predicted, nothing really changed and nothing extraordinary happened. She learned some mildly interesting things at school. In history class, she read about an explorer named Magellan who seemed to travel around the world almost as much as Lucy did. In science class, she learned about the solar system and how all of the planets revolved around the sun. Again, this reminded Cornelia of her mother.

After school each day, she walked home alone, and once at home, she fended off Madame Desjardins with her arsenal of words. Her favorite new word for the housekeeper was "hamadryad," which meant "Abyssinian baboon." From her *Superior Person's Book of Words,* she also learned some new words she could direct at Walter if he went overboard with the teasing, such as "fopdoo-dle" ("a fool"), "galoot" ("a clumsy oaf"), or "pilgarlic" ("a poor bald-headed man who presents a sorry spectacle").

Lucy returned home from her trip, and with her came a caravan of luggage. She kissed Cornelia distract-edly, and then swept into the study and talked on the phone for hours. Apparently her concert had not gone well, and she was in a sour mood for days. She spent hours smoking sullenly in the music room, missing meals and tinkering with new music pieces. Everyone—even Ingrid—tiptoed around the apartment so Lucy would not be disturbed.

Late Monday afternoon, Lucy called Cornelia into the music room. Cornelia apprehensively walked into her mother's sanctuary.

Lucy sat at the keyboard of the piano, smoking. The light from outside shone on her harshly beautiful fea-tures. She kept her shoulder-length jet-black hair cut in a line so straight that it could have been used as a ruler. Long, muscular arms connected her famously wide hands and shoulders. Even though she was a pe-tite woman, she always tilted her strong chin upward, giving her the appearance of an empress gazing down on her subject. People from magazines and newspapers always wanted to shoot pictures of Lucy like that, sitting regally at her *Bête Noire.*

"Come in, darling. Sit next to me for a minute," Lucy said, patting the seat of the bench in front of the piano. It was the only place to sit in the room besides the floor. Cornelia moved some music sheets to the floor and dutifully sat down next to her mother.

"Did you miss me while I was in Russia?" Lucy asked, smoothing down Cornelia's hair somewhat awkwardly.

"Yes," said Cornelia uneasily, feeling as dull and sedentary as a turnip compared to her mother.

"Well, I had a dreadful time," Lucy replied, smoothing her own hair down now. "My concert was ghastly, and I had the longest trip home ever. They lost my luggage not once, but *twice.* I need a rest. I might go to the beach house for a few days and relax."

Cornelia nodded silently and thumbed one of the keys on the keyboard in front of her. She already knew what her mother was going to say next. As if on cue, Lucy got up and closed the doors to the music room.

"Cornelia," she began in a low voice. "I know that Madame Desjardins can be bothersome sometimes, and that you like your privacy. But she's been very upset about her relationship with you lately." She suppressed a little sideways smile. "You're not casting spells on her with your long words, are you?"

"She never leaves me alone," Cornelia mumbled, not daring to look at Lucy. "It's the only way to make her go away."

"Well, I'm sure that she just wants to help," Lucy said, sitting down next to Cornelia again. "We worry about you getting lonely, that's all. Why don't you make friends with some of the other girls at school?"

Cornelia didn't even bother to address Lucy's boring question. "Can I come to the beach house with you?" she asked instead, already knowing the answer.

"No, darling. You have to go to school," Lucy said. There was a moment of silence. "Cornelia, I've been thinking. Would you like to take piano lessons?"

"No," Cornelia answered, her voice quavering a bit. It was not the first time they'd had this discussion.

"Why not?" Lucy said with genuine interest. "You know that I would never pressure you, but I'm always curious why you're not interested. I'm sure you'd be superb. You certainly have the genes for it."

Cornelia frowned. This conversation was not going well. She knew why she didn't want to take lessons: it would just trap her in her mother's long shadow even more. She much preferred books to music, because words made up *her* private world, and hers alone. Her mastery of words was the only thing that made her Cornelia S. Englehart, and not just Lucy Englehart's Daughter. But of course, she couldn't say this to her mother.

"I just don't *want* to," she said stubbornly. She tried to change the subject. "Can I come with you on one of your concert trips soon?"

"When you're older," her mother replied, and lit another cigarette. She looked at Cornelia for a minute and deliberated. "All right. Now, run out so I can work on this Rachmaninoff piece. It's driving me insane. My hands need to be about an inch wider than they already are to really do it right."

Cornelia walked solemnly to the door when her mother said, "And I'll see you this weekend when I get back. Be good, darling." She was already studying the sheet music on the piano.

And that was that.

All of that waiting, thought Cornelia indignantly, *and the only time she talks to me, it's about Madame Desjardins and piano lessons.*

She grew cross and vowed to use even more confusing and complex words as revenge. Her mother left the next morning.

When Cornelia came home after school later that week, a big moving truck was parked outside the building. Boxes littered the sidewalk, waiting to be moved in.

"Top of the day t' you, Miss Cornelia," yelled Walter across the lobby. "Blimey—look at this mess! You 'ave a new next-door neighbor. Them movers must be barmy to leave boxes laying about outside on the pavement. All the dogs living in this building might take 'em for new square fire hydrants."

Cornelia smiled. A few minutes later, Madame Desjardins let her into the apartment, and she ran up to her bedroom immediately. Strangely, she found that she had no interest in reading. Nothing in her bedroom interested her, not even the contentious word book. She felt anxious for some reason, like something was about to happen, but she didn't know what.

She shocked Madame Desjardins by coming downstairs before dinner and ambling around the apartment. She fiddled with the stereo in the living room until Madame Desjardins discovered her, let out a shriek, and sent Cornelia scuttling away. After that, Cornelia set up a game of checkers in the apartment's main hallway, playing both sides. But then Madame Desjardins came swishing out of the kitchen, didn't see the operation taking place on the floor, and stepped on the board. She even slid a few feet, scattering the black and red plastic disks everywhere.

By five o'clock, Madame Desjardins's nerves were shot.

"*Mon Dieu!* One day, you hide in your room like a secret, and the next day, you are everywhere! I step on you wherever I put my foot," she wailed.

But it was Cornelia's description of Madame Desjardins's *coq au vin* cooking in the kitchen as "mephitical" (which meant "stinking, noxious") that sent the housekeeper over the edge.

"Out! Outside with you!" she exclaimed. She vehemently shook Cornelia's coat and beckoned for her to put it on. She put some money into one of Cornelia's pockets to get "some little cakes from that place" for her dessert that night. "Not that you deserve little cakes today," Madame Desjardins muttered, glaring at Cornelia as she shoved her into the hallway.

The door thudded shut behind Cornelia. Boxes lined the walls of the corridor, ready to be hauled into the new neighbor's home next door. As Cornelia passed the front door of the apartment, she noticed a small blue sign hammered onto it, just above the doorknob. She leaned in to examine it. The sign proclaimed in white letters:

Attention! Chien Bizarre.

Cornelia blinked. What did it mean? She got into the elevator and mulled it over on her way down to the lobby.

She went on her errand to the Magnolia Bakery, dragging along because the trip had been a punishment. She took an extra-long time coming home just to make Madame Desjardins worry about her.

It was dark when Cornelia strolled back to her building. Walter wasn't at the front desk, and the quietness of the lobby unnerved her even more. When she got out of the elevator on her floor, she glanced again at the mysterious blue sign on her neighbor's front door.

Suddenly the door opened and something shot out of the apartment. It ran full speed over her feet, and she staggered backward in surprise.

"Gah!!" a man shouted from inside the apartment. "Mister Kinyatta!! You little beast! Come back here immediately!"

And into the hallway ran a short, bearded, dark man wearing a turban and a knee-length shirt over trousers.

"Hello, young miss," he huffed in Cornelia's direction, and scrambled down the hallway in pursuit of the creature. "Mister Kinyatta, come *here* or I'll put you in a stew!" the man hollered as he ran and disappeared around the corner.

Cornelia followed him and peeked around the corner to see what was happening. The object in question appeared to be a small black French bulldog, who was very crafty and fast and clearly not ready to be marched back into the apartment. Every time the man leaped for Mister Kinyatta, the dog darted past him and wheeled around like a tiny bull, challenging the man to lunge for him again.

"Ugh!" groaned the man to Cornelia. His turban had shifted sideways on his head. "He looks like a clown but he is really a little devil! He taunts everyone except Virginia-ji, especially me." The dog was so excited by now that his eyes seemed to be going in opposite directions. "Come here, Mister Kinyatta!" the man bellowed helplessly.

"I know how to get him back into the apartment," Cornelia said. This was practically a speech for her, since she barely uttered a word to people she knew—much less to a stranger. She rustled the bag from the Magnolia Bakery and Mister Kinyatta snapped to attention.

"Oooh—what is it—food?" the little man cried hopefully. "He *loves* food."

Mister Kinyatta stood a few feet from Cornelia, looking her up and down. His ears stood up on his head like boat sails. Cornelia rattled the bag again, opening it a little bit and showing the dog what was inside.

"Mmmmmmm," she said enticingly. "Cupcakes." Mister Kinyatta took a few steps toward her, licking his chops. Cornelia backed up toward the apartment, and the dog followed her. By the time she had triumphantly lured Mister Kinyatta into the apartment, the dog was running around her ankles and leaping up into the air.

The man marched in after them. Now that the situation was under control, he assumed an air of authority.

"Bring him into the kitchen, miss!" he instructed importantly. "Yes! Very good!" He reached up and straightened
his turban.

As soon as all three of them were in the kitchen, the
man reached into a ceramic jar that teetered on top of
several unopened moving boxes and extracted a treat
for Mister Kinyatta. He threw it across the kitchen floor
and the dog ran after it.

"Quick—run out of the kitchen!" the man yelled,
pointing theatrically toward the corridor. He and Cornelia ran out into the hallway, and the man snapped a
gate into place in the doorframe behind them, trapping
Mister Kinyatta in the kitchen.

The man stood next to Cornelia. He ran his fingers
through his beard and smoothed down his shirt. Now that
they were standing side by side, Cornelia noticed that
he was only a bit taller than she was. She thought that
he must have been Madame Desjardins's age, around
sixty years old.

"Thank you very much, young miss," the man managed to say after a minute. "He is usually crazy, but not
this crazy. He is very excited about the move."

Cornelia nodded, but then she got distracted by the
apartment around her. It was very similar to her big
white echoing home next door—but even with all of the
moving boxes still littered around it, the space already
seemed completely different, even fascinating. Several

enormous potted palm trees stood in a makeshift forest in the living room at the end of the corridor. In the corridor, dozens of silk pillows were stacked in brightly colored towers, and some of them spilled like a luxurious waterfall onto the floor. Amidst the pillows lay a wonderful old-fashioned record player with a big horn, a warped record spinning lazily on its turntable. At the end of the hallway loomed a huge bronze statue of a woman wearing an elaborate headpiece and holding a strange musical instrument. It was beautiful and frightening to Cornelia at the same time.

The man followed Cornelia's gaze. "That is Virginia-ji's statue of Saraswati, the Hindu goddess of knowledge and the arts. It came all the way from India," he said. "By the way, I am Patel."

Cornelia nodded, her usual shyness stealing back into her. "It was nice to meet you," she said, turning to leave. "I'm late for dinner."

Just at that moment, a willowy old woman opened the front door and walked in. She carried several shopping bags and was putting her keys into her small silk purse. She didn't see Cornelia and the man standing there.

"Patel, I'm home," she called out tiredly. She took off her gloves and started unbuttoning her elegant black coat. A silk scarf covered her hair. Patel walked over to help her with her coat and packages.

"We have a guest," he announced as he ferried her coat off to the front closet.

"Oh. Hello," said the woman, noticing Cornelia for the first time. "Who are you?"

She had the most lovely, radiant face, even though wrinkles surrounded her eyes. She wore a floor-length silk dress and several long strands of pearls. Glistening rings adorned her fingers. She was very thin and pale, and seemed to Cornelia to belong to a different era, when people took only black-and-white pictures.

"I'm Cornelia S. Englehart," Cornelia replied.

She was torn now: on one hand, she knew that Madame Desjardins was probably wringing her hands and calling the police because she had been gone for so long. On the other hand, this woman seemed so compelling and warm that Cornelia—for the first time in her life—wanted to stay a little while.

"From next door," Patel offered from afar, his voice muffled in the coat closet.

"What a charming name," the woman said. "I am Virginia Somerset. Patel and I and Mister Kinyatta are your new neighbors."

"The beast ran into the hall, and this smart girl lured him back into the kitchen with her bag of food," Patel informed Virginia helpfully as he reappeared at her side. Mister Kinyatta heard his mistress's voice and leaped up and down behind his gate.

"How clever of you, Cornelia S. Thank goodness you reined him in, for I don't know what I'd do with myself if he ran away," Virginia said, reaching over the gate and stroking his head with great affection. Strangely, the dog began to make purring noises. Cornelia listened in surprise, completely enraptured by this odd little animal.

"Cornelia-ji was leaving to go home," Patel said. "She is late for dinner."

Virginia smiled, deepening the friendly creases around her eyes. "One should never be late for dinner," she said, looking down at Cornelia and her bakery bag. "Especially when there are Magnolia cupcakes for dessert. But before you go, tell me: Do you like books, by any chance?"

Cornelia nodded.

"Well, then," Virginia said. "You must visit with us when we're done unpacking. I have the most wonderful library. Everyone falls in love with it. It's like a field of poppies—no one ever wants to leave. Come by for a cup of tea soon, and I'll show it to you."

"Do you have dictionaries?" Cornelia blurted out, and then wished she hadn't.

"Why, of course," Virginia answered. "And in many languages as well." She and Patel looked quizzically at their guest.

Cornelia's face reddened. "It was very nice to meet you," she said, and walked to the door. Patel escorted her out.

"Maybe you will come and keep Virginia-ji company sometime," he said as Cornelia stepped into the hallway. "You should know that she does not ask everyone, although there are many who want invitations," he added gravely. "Good night," he said. With a slight bow, he began to close the door.

"Wait!" said Cornelia.

Patel peeked out again. "Yes?"

"What does it mean?" Cornelia asked, pointing to the blue sign above the doorknob.

Patel leaned around the door to gaze at it. "Ah," he said, tapping the sign with his fingernail. "*Chien bizarre.* It means 'a bizarre dog lives here.' And now you know this is true. Good night, Cornelia-ji."

And with that, Patel shut the door, closing Cornelia off from the unusual world inside.

Madame Desjardins was busy harassing the staff at the Magnolia Bakery on the phone when Cornelia walked in.

"I do not care if you have cakes to make! Go out and look for her right away! Search the streets!" she shouted. Then, mid-sentence, the housekeeper saw Cornelia standing there. She slammed the phone down on the cradle and burst into tears.

"*Eiiiieeeeeeeeeeeeeeee!* Cornelia Street Englehart! Where have you *been*? You make me age ten years in the last hour!!! Look at me! I am an old lady now—with a weak heart!" Madame Desjardins howled. This went on for quite some time.

Yet later that evening, as they ate the *coq au vin* chicken stew together for dinner (which, by the way, was very good, despite the way Cornelia had slandered it earlier), Madame Desjardins calmed down enough to notice something different about Cornelia. She didn't seem as withdrawn; nor did she speak in strange tongues as she had been doing lately. Madame Desjardins's first inclination was to worry about the change. And then she decided to enjoy this unexpected gift instead of questioning where it came from.

Later that evening, after she'd tucked Cornelia into bed, the housekeeper took a break from watching *Gone with the Wind* on television and tiptoed down the upstairs hallway.

For the first time in a long time, she didn't hear Cornelia crying behind her closed bedroom door.

Chapter Three

Virginia

Several weeks went by. Lucy left again, this time on vacation (a "retreat," she called it) in Morocco, a country on the northwest coast of Africa (as Cornelia learned from checking a big atlas in the school library). On her way out the door, Lucy promised to send a crate of presents, of "rugs and silver and I don't know—gorgeous things." Cornelia's mouth made a hard little line when she heard this. She wouldn't be fooled again by any boxes coming to the apartment from foreign countries.

Madame Desjardins never had a cross word for or about her employer, but Cornelia overheard her talking to Walter about Lucy. Cornelia walked into the lobby after school one afternoon and saw the two of them conspiring over the front desk.

"She is never home," Madame Desjardins whispered to Walter, "and now Cornelia Street is growing up without a mother *or* a father. She sees more of Madame Lucille on the cover of a CD than in their home."

Then both Walter and Madame Desjardins shook their heads tragically. When Madame Desjardins saw Cornelia standing there listening, she exclaimed, *"Zut alors!"* and swept the girl upstairs. Neither of them mentioned the incident again.

Cornelia thought constantly about Virginia, Patel, and Mister Kinyatta. The moving boxes in the hallway had long since been taken into the apartment next door, reemerged empty, and been thrown away. Then for several weeks, dusty workers went in and out of Virginia's apartment, carrying toolboxes, crowbars, electric saws, and lots of marble slabs. Cornelia and Madame Desjardins heard the sound of hammers tapping and drills whirring and heavy furniture being arranged. But the building was old and the walls thick, so they didn't hear or see much else once the initial fanfare was over.

Shyness prevented Cornelia from visiting her neighbors again. She knew that she was being silly—after all, Virginia and Patel had both given her special invitations to stop by—but she couldn't help it. While she tried to overcome her bashfulness, Cornelia thought about the world next door when she went to sleep at night and again when she woke up in the morning. She was filled with questions. What had been in all of those hundreds of boxes? And those palm trees—where had they all come from, and why did Virginia and Patel need them? To grow coconuts? But why would they need to grow coconuts when they could just buy them in a store? Did Virginia have lots of beds in there, and if not, then why did they need so many silk pillows?

Finally, a combination of bursting curiosity and sheer boredom made Cornelia put aside her timidity and ring Virginia Somerset's doorbell. It was Monday, February 19—Presidents' Day—and Cornelia had the day off from school. It had rained all weekend—an ugly late-winter rain. Madame Desjardins was near despair, since Cornelia had been stuck inside and underfoot the whole time.

Today, however, the cold downpours stopped after lunch, and Cornelia immediately tugged on her boots as if she were going outside. She galloped into the study, where Madame Desjardins giggled at the cartoons in the *New York Post*.

"Can I go for a walk?" Cornelia asked.

Madame Desjardins jumped with surprise behind her newspaper and gave her ward immediate permission to go.

Cornelia closed the front door to her apartment and ambled over to Virginia's door. Before she could lose her nerve again, she reached out and rang the bell. Soft foot-steps approached the door on the other side.

"Yes?" said Patel as he peered out. "Oh! Cornelia-from-next-door." He saw her coat and boots. "You were outside in this monstrous weather?" Cornelia nodded piteously. "Would you like a cup of tea with Virginia-ji to warm up?" Cornelia nodded again, and Patel let her in.

"Virginia-ji will be most delighted to see you," Patel told Cornelia as she pulled off her boots in the front foyer. "Come with me."

Cornelia followed him in her stockinged feet down the corridor. All of the doors to the rooms along the way were closed. Long velvet curtains covered the far end of the hallway, concealing the living room on the other side.

"Cornelia-ji to visit," Patel announced as he grandly opened the curtains over the entrance to the living room. Cornelia entered the room, and a wave of amaze-ment washed over her. She couldn't believe that her fa-miliar apartment was just thirty feet away on the other side of the wall, for this room was surely as exotic as Lucy's Moroccan retreat.

Before she could help herself, Cornelia counted the palm trees. Eight, nine, twelve, fifteen . . . twenty in all! And they were actually planted right *in* the floor itself. The trees sloped majestically above the entrance to the room and framed a huge arched window in the far wall. The palm fronds softened the light coming in from outside and cast intricate shadow patterns on the floor (which, by the way, was *not* made from wood like the floors in Cornelia's apartment, but rather cool white marble tiles). Colored-glass lanterns swung lazily from the branches, occasionally glinting in the sunlight like rubies, emeralds, sapphires, and diamonds.

In the middle of this forest, under a canopy of fronds, sat a Moroccan daybed with tall, curving sides, like an Arabian sleigh. The silk pillows that Cornelia remembered made opulent piles on top of the bed, and dozens more of them were scattered throughout the room. Underneath the bed lay the thickest, most luxurious Oriental carpet Cornelia had ever seen. It stretched out like a silken bed of grass beneath the palm branches.

And in the middle of the room, in the middle of that wonderful bed, was Virginia Somerset, deeply absorbed in a book.

She wore another long, flowing dress and her fingers sparkled with jewels. A scarf woven from gold filaments wreathed her hair. She looked up from her book and smiled when she saw Cornelia. Her cheekbones curved into huge half-moons. She looked like a wise, glamorous countess.

"Cornelia S. Englehart," Virginia said. "How good of you to come. I was just about to have some tea—would you like to join me?" She patted the daybed and said, "Patel, mint tea, please."

Patel nodded. "Of course," he said, and whooshed out through the curtains.

Cornelia was sure that few princesses had ever luxuriated on a daybed as gorgeous as Virginia's. She strolled through the palm tree forest and climbed up amongst the pillows, next to her hostess. It was wonderfully comfortable. Cornelia smiled shyly at Virginia and looked around the rest of the room. Even the walls were covered in white marble.

"Do you like it?" Virginia asked enthusiastically. Cornelia nodded. "It took the workmen a few weeks to do it, but I'm so pleased with the results. It was modeled after a garden in a Moroccan palace that I stayed in with my sisters, a long time ago."

"It's the most beautiful room I've ever seen," said Cornelia.

Virginia nodded. "Well, just wait. It's not even done yet. I'm having a real fountain built in the middle of the room," she said. "But we need new pipes in the floor to make it gurgle and run, and that's going to take *forever*. I have a fountain ready to go, of course." She pointed to a large marble object in the far corner.

Cornelia thought for a second. "I have an idea," she said. "Why don't you make it into sort of a wishing well, with a filter instead of running water? And you can put fish in it. Big goldfish." Even Cornelia was surprised to hear herself talking so much.

"That's not a bad idea," Virginia replied. "And I love the idea of having big, fat orange goldfish in my fountain. Those dashes of bright color. You can see why the artist Matisse wanted to paint them all the time. What a lovely man. He painted a portrait of my mother as well, years and years ago."

Cornelia was very pleased that Virginia approved of her idea about the fountain. Emboldened, she asked, "Can I walk through the rest of the room?"

"Of course!" Virginia exclaimed. "I want people to traipse around in it and enjoy it! That's what all of the rooms in my home were *designed* for. Each room represents a different country where I have lived. Morocco, for example. And I have the most wonderful French drawing room—blue and gold and daintily upright. I also built a dark, grand English library. You can't *help* but be smarter once you've spent time inside it. But my favorite room of all is my bedroom, modeled after a room in an Indian palace. It should be in a museum, if I do say so myself. Someday you can see all of them. But I'm afraid that I'm too weary to give you a tour today.

"Cornelia, it's nice to be back in New York," she added. "Lovely to be home. I've been away for a very long time." She sighed sadly.

"My mother has been away for a very long time too," answered Cornelia. She peered into the fountain. "And she is also always in different places. She's a pianist and is always playing someplace that's not New York."

A look of recognition came over Virginia's face. "Ohhhh," she said, as though she had solved a mystery. "Is your mother Lucille Englehart?"

"Yes," Cornelia said, sorry now that she had brought it up. It always made her testy when adults spoke reverently about Lucy.

"Hmmm. Remarkable. I have heard her play before, many times," Virginia said. "Where is she today, Cornelia?" she asked.

"Morocco. At a 'retreat.'"

"What a coincidence!" exclaimed Virginia, rearranging the pillows around herself. "And here you are, in my Moroccan room, having an adventure of your own. Tell me, do you have any other ideas to make this room even better? Your idea about the fountain is going to change everything in here. Maybe I'll hire you as my decorator."

To Cornelia's surprise, tears of gratitude welled up in her eyes. Usually when people found out who Lucy was, they were no longer interested in Cornelia or her ideas. They only wanted to know more about Lucy, and what it was like being her daughter, and what their apartment was like, and what Lucy ate for breakfast and that sort of thing. And now, in Virginia's Moroccan forest, Cornelia suddenly became an interesting, independent person for the first time in her life.

"I'll think about it," she said.

Yet she knew immediately that she wouldn't want to change a thing about either the room or its owner.

In a few minutes, Patel reemerged through the curtains with a gleaming silver tray heaped with glasses, spoons, sugar, and a teapot of steaming tea. The clean, soothing smell of mint filled the room. Then came the approaching click of dog toenails behind the door curtains.

"Gah!" cried Patel as he gingerly placed the tea tray on a little table next to the daybed. "How did he get out of the kitchen?" The curtains swayed around the bottom, and Mister Kinyatta emerged victoriously through the part in the center.

"Mister Kinyatta! You are the worst, most presumptuous creature I have ever met!" Patel snapped. "This tea is *not* for you!" He leaped toward the dog and they immediately started running in circles around the room. Cornelia gleefully dodged Mister Kinyatta on his first lap.

"Patel," cried Virginia. "Don't worry—I'll take care of him. Mister Kinyatta! Pay attention!"

The dog screeched to a halt and looked at her.

"I bet *someone* would like to come up on the bed, wouldn't he?" Virginia said slyly. Mister Kinyatta trotted up to the edge of the daybed, still keeping an eye on Patel.

"Cornelia, can you help Mister Kinyatta up here? He

thinks that he's a lot bigger than he actually is," said Virginia. Mister Kinyatta clearly understood his owner, for he looked at Cornelia expectantly.

"Let him sniff your hand," Virginia suggested. "Mister Kinyatta, do you remember Cornelia? She brought you cupcakes a few weeks ago." She paused, then said, "Oh, maybe I shouldn't remind him about that, since he didn't actually get any of the cupcakes in the end, did he?"

The dog looked suspiciously at Cornelia as she knelt down next to him. After appraising her for a few moments, he seemed to find her acceptable and gave her an arrogant little lick. Cornelia lifted him up and put him neatly in the middle of the daybed.

"He is the most spoiled dog in the Western Hemisphere," Patel grumbled.

He walked over to what looked like a leather suitcase and opened it up, revealing the antique record player Cornelia had seen on her first visit. He attached the big horn to it.

"This is very old," Patel informed Cornelia. "You used to have to wind it up. But we fixed it so you could plug it into the wall, like a toaster or something."

He looked through a pile of old records stacked next to the machine, pulling out a few discs and considering each one carefully. "Mozart," he said to himself, placing a record on the turntable and switching it on. The sound of pops and scratches soon came out of the machine as the record warmed up. In a few seconds, they heard the first tinny strands of a Mozart symphony. Satisfied, Patel got up, poured tea into two little etched glasses on the tray, and left the room.

"Why does Patel sometimes call you Virginia-ji, and call me Cornelia-ji?" Cornelia asked when the coast was clear.

"Patel-ji is from India," Virginia answered. "In that country, when you add the suffix 'ji' to someone's name, it's a sign of affection. I say it all the time without thinking—sometimes even to women in stores and waiters.

"You know, a friend of mine gave me a big, fancy stereo a few years ago," she sighed, changing the subject. She lay back on the pillows, listening to the music for a few moments with her eyes closed. "It had a thousand buttons and huge speakers and probably cost as much as a car. But I couldn't get used to it. In fact, I disliked it. The music sounded too clear to me. Doesn't that sound silly? But I don't have any memories attached to music that sounds like that—at least, not in my home. I like listening to music *this* way, on an old record player. That's how I used to listen to music with my sisters when we were young, like you." She opened her eyes.

"How many sisters do you have?" Cornelia asked politely.

"Three of them. Alexandra and Beatrice were twins. Gladys was the plump one," Virginia smiled naughtily. "And I was the youngest of the four. Actually, there's a picture of us, over there, if you want to see what they looked like." She pointed to an old black-and-white photo on a low shelf across the room.

It was a lovely picture of four young ladies sitting with great poise in a room very much like Virginia's palm court. The first three ladies were slender and elegant, with long necks, and the fourth was plump and impish-looking. Wonderful, nearly matching hats perched on their heads, and the sisters toasted one another with Moroccan tea glasses. Grinning men in white robes and dark caps with flat tops and tassles surrounded their table.

Cornelia examined the picture with great interest. Since she was an only child, other people's brothers and sisters fascinated her. The very idea of siblings was novel. The ladies in this photo reminded her of three swans and one big quacking goose. She looked at their faces and detected a young and pretty Virginia under one of the old-fashioned hats.

"Do your sisters live in New York as well?" Cornelia asked.

"No," said Virginia sadly. "I'm the only one left."

Cornelia didn't know what to say. The room was silent for a moment, until Virginia continued, "We were in Morocco when that picture was taken. We grew up here in New York, and lived in a big apartment on Fifth Avenue with a butler and lots of maids. Not bad, of course, but we were *so* restless. It was hard being a girl back in those days. You got watched and chaperoned and had to behave nicely all the time. All of those white gloves and manners! We couldn't get away with *anything*, Cornelia. That was especially tough on Gladys, who was such a tomboy. So as soon as we were old enough to travel without our governess, we left to see the world. Anywhere and everywhere a train or a boat or a plane could take us. Or even a bicycle or camel or horse."

Cornelia couldn't quite believe this. She always thought that it was the parents who traveled, leaving behind their children, not the other way around.

"How did you get your parents to let you go?" she asked. "If I'm gone for more than an hour, our house-keeper calls every store in the neighborhood."

Virginia smiled. "Well, we had to be very crafty about it. You see, most girls didn't go to college back then. But we pleaded and begged and told our parents that we needed *some* sort of an education before we got married. We told them that we wanted to study the art and customs of many different countries so we would have more interesting things to talk about at parties and to suitors when we got back. I don't think we ever really fooled our mother, but Gladys badgered our father so much that he finally said yes.

"Our poor father," she continued mischievously. "All he wanted was a son. And he kept getting daughters, one after another. When there were no sons, all he wanted was a son-in-law. He couldn't wait for us to get married, and then none of us ever did."

"Why not?" asked Cornelia. Although only mildly rebellious herself, she still wanted to hear about any and all forms of rebellion against non-understanding parents.

"We didn't see any reason to," Virginia answered. "The Somerset sisters were *always* together and we were *never* lonely as a result. No one ever met Alexandra's standards for Beatrice, and vice versa. Gladys was too robust and she was always getting into trouble.

"And as for me—well, all my life, I've somehow frightened people away with my flashy vocabulary," she continued. "I'm a writer and storyteller, and therefore words are very important to me. But people get intimidated sometimes when you use long words, and run away. So the very thing that made me special also has always had the potential to make me lonely. On the other hand, this talent can also be *very* useful in deflecting unpleasant or vexing people."

"I know exactly what you mean!" Cornelia exclaimed. "Our housekeeper, Madame Desjardins, is always buzzing around me like a bee. The only way I can get any privacy is to use longer and longer words until she gets mad and goes away," she explained.

"Aha," Virginia said. "So you too practice the art of parisology. A very smart weapon when one encounters a person who is multiloquous, or when you are subjected to bavardage."

Cornelia was stumped. "What?" she asked. Ironically, she almost found herself saying *"Comment?"* like Madame Desjardins.

Virginia laughed again. "'Parisology' is when you use words that are unnecessarily complicated so that no one understands what you're talking about. 'Multiloquous' means 'very talkative,' and 'bavardage,' which is one of my favorite words, means 'foolish or empty chatter.'"

Cornelia was a little bit daunted. "Those are good words," she said. "I didn't know any of them."

"Not many people know those words, so don't feel bad. Anyway, I can tell that you're very smart. I wasn't a parisology master until later in life." Virginia studied her young guest with admiration for a minute.

"I wish that I could go on a trip around the world," Cornelia sighed. "But I bet I'd have to take Madame Desjardins too. How old were you when you got to go?"

"We left on our voyage when I was twenty years old, in 1949. Alexandra and Beatrice were twenty-two and

Gladys was twenty-one. We called ourselves the Somerset Adventuresses. And interestingly, the first stop of our voyage was in Marrakech, a city in Morocco." Virginia looked wistful for a moment. "Would you like to hear a story about some of our time there? You can imagine your mother there as well, maybe even doing the same things."

Cornelia peered at the faces in the photo again. The Somerset sisters indeed looked vivacious and defiant and extremely happy to be where they were. For a moment, the room around Cornelia seemed to turn black and white and she thought she could hear the voices of the ladies and their servants. She looked at Virginia.

"Yes, please," she said.

Virginia reached out for a glass of tea. Long mint leaves had unfurled inside the glasses on the silver tray. She handed one to Cornelia and took one for herself.

"One should always toast before drinking, Cornelia," Virginia said ceremoniously. "To conversations, as opposed to foolish chatter," she declared, holding her glass up to clink it with Cornelia's. "And to adventure."

She took a sip, and began to tell her story.

Chapter Four

Morocco, 1949

"It took us a long time to get to Morocco. First we took a huge ocean liner called the *Mauretania II* from New York to England. And by the time we got off the ship, the crew members and the captain could not have been happier to see us go, for every single night, Gladys would clean them out in poker games. Even if the games lasted until three in the morning, the next day she would always join us for breakfast, looking as innocent as a nun.

"Then we had our trunks and bags hoisted onto another, smaller ship, and sailed down to Portugal. From there, we caught a third ship, which took us from Europe to Africa. We finally arrived in Casablanca, one of the famous port cities in Morocco.

"None of us had ever seen anything like it. You and I are used to American cities, with all of those skyscrapers and cement, with taxis darting around us and subways shaking the ground below our feet.

"Casablanca was completely different. From the moment you set foot on the land, the most wonderful chaos surrounded you. Hundreds of people filled the streets, selling things, running about, shouting to one another. Dust swirled in the air like smoke. Small, square buildings, most of them made out of white clay, lined the streets instead of tall steel towers. Dry palm trees baked under the hot sun, and the strong smells of fish and cooking lamb wafted up from the market stalls along the docks. Dozens of dirty braying donkeys pulled carts up and down the roads, driven along by barefoot boys or men with long robes and red hats with flat tops and tassels called fezzes."

Cornelia pointed to one of the servants in the photo of Virginia and her sisters. "Is he wearing a fez?" she asked.

Virginia squinted at it. "Yes," she answered. "I love those little hats, but they've always looked terrible on me. On our first night in Morocco, Gladys won a fez from a hotel manager in a card game of fan-tan. She wore it all the time, until it blew away in a sandstorm."

She continued her story.

"French soldiers idled about in the streets and cafés. At the time, France ruled the country, although

Morocco still had an important sultan whose family had been ruling the country for centuries.

"Our trip wasn't over when we got off the ship. Right away, we boarded an old train already overflowing with people and even a few animals. We sweltered in the heat until Gladys opened the window of our compartment. So much dust flew in that our faces grew gray and we couldn't breathe. We closed it again and fanned ourselves with our tickets for the rest of the journey. I had never been so filthy, and let me tell you, Cornelia, it was *wonderful.*

"We finally pulled into the train station in the city of Marrakech, where we planned to live for several months. We opened the train's door to the platform and stumbled out, happy to stretch our legs at last. People streamed off the other cars around us.

"When the cloud of dust finally settled down, a young man stepped forward to greet us. His skin was the color of hazelnuts, and a long robe draped his tall, skinny frame. A fez sat neatly on his head, and he wore an amused look on his face.

"'Miss Somerset?' he asked.

"'Yes,' all four of us replied in unison.

"'*Marhaba,*' he said graciously, nodding to each of us in turn. '*Ismi* Pierre. I am Pierre. I am your guide in Marrakech. *Ahlan wa sahlan,*' he added."

"What does A-ha-lon wa sa-ha-lon mean?" interrupted Cornelia, stumbling over the new words.

"It means 'Welcome' in Arabic," said Virginia. "Although we had no idea at the time. He could have been saying 'I'm going to cook you for dinner' and we wouldn't have known the difference."

"Now, months before, our mother had written ahead to a travel agency and rented a magnificent Moroccan house for the four of us. Pierre was one of the servants who would live with us and help us while we were there.

"'Follow me, *min fadlik*,' Pierre said, which meant 'please,' and we followed him out of the railroad station. A grand but disheveled old car waited for us outside.

"'I will follow with the luggage and meet you at home very soon, *inshallah*,' Pierre said, opening the back door of the car for us. I learned later that *inshallah* meant 'God willing.' 'This is your driver, Ahmed, and he will take you to the *medina*, the old city, where your house is.'

"Alexandra and Beatrice looked worriedly back at our trunks and suitcases piled up on the sidewalk of the station.

"'I wonder if we'll ever see them again,' Alexandra said, but she climbed into the car anyway. The rest of us trundled in after her.

"We drove slowly through a labyrinth of ancient winding, narrow streets lined with low ramshackle buildings. Ahmed made a great racket, honking at every person or donkey that got in our way. People peered into the windows at us and even tapped on the glass. Once while the car was stopped at an intersection, an old man tried to sell Gladys a smelly goat, but Ahmed leaned out his window and yelled at him until he went away.

"Finally, the car turned onto a deserted street and parked in front of a splintery-looking, filthy old building. From the outside, it looked like it might crumble into dust if you even touched it. Ahmed turned off the car, popped out, and opened the back door for us.

"'*Ahlan wa sahlan,*' Ahmed said. My sisters and I looked at each other in confusion.

"'*Hina, hina,*' Ahmed said, meaning 'Here, here.' He smiled and pointed to the door. '*Beyt,*' he added. 'Home.'

"Alexandra opened her purse and pulled out a piece of paper from the travel agency with an address written on it. She showed it to Ahmed, who nodded vigorously. '*Aywah!* Yes!' he exclaimed. '*Hina!*' He began to pull our hand luggage out of the trunk.

"'This can't be right,' Alexandra stammered. 'Our mother would never stick us in such a dump! What should we do?' She helplessly started flipping through her Arabic phrase book. A broken shutter swung in the warm breeze, creaking on its rusty hinges.

"Beatrice took control of the situation. 'What about the photos they sent us? The descriptions? A Moroccan palace, indeed!' she hissed. 'Give me that!' she said, and snatched at the phrase book. She marched up to Ahmed, who was lugging our bags to the front door.

"'*Inwehn* . . . umm . . . *ghalat,*' she told him, trying to say 'Wrong address.' She found another word that worked for her. 'Aha!' she shouted. '*Uteel!*'

"'What does that mean?' Gladys asked her.

"'Hotel, I hope,' Beatrice said, and began dragging the bags back into the trunk.

"'What do you mean, *hotel*?' shouted Alexandra. 'He just has the wrong address. Our mother went through all of that trouble to rent the house, and we're going to find it! Give me back that book!'

"Gladys gave a loud sigh of disgust and pushed past us. She stomped up to the front door of the house and knocked noisily on it. The door opened and a young boy in a white robe appeared in the doorway.

"'*Ahlan,*' he said to Gladys, and she disappeared into the house. My stomach almost turned over, for I was sure that the house would collapse on top of her.

"After what seemed like the longest few minutes in the history of the world, she reappeared at the door and peered out at us.

"'Come in, you fools,' she said. 'We're in the right place.' She stalked out, grabbed her purse from the trunk, nodded at Ahmed, and went back inside.

"Beatrice cleared her throat and exclaimed, 'What is she *doing*?'

"Overcome by curiosity, I followed Gladys into

the tattered-looking house. The boy still stood at the front door, holding it open for me. *'Ahlan,'* he repeated politely as I walked through the door into the house.

"To my astonishment, the inside was absolutely nothing like the outside. Night and day could not have been more different. I had expected to find a disgusting house filled with spiders and rotting wood and who knows what, or who, inside.

"But instead, I walked into a gleaming blue and white palace, fresh and cool as spring water. Towering palm trees grew right out of the marble floor, which is where I got the idea for this living room, and dozens of colored-glass lanterns dangled above our heads. Powerful white pillars soared up to the high ceiling, which was made of thick glass. During the day, the piercing blue Moroccan sky and sunlight shone through it, and after sunset, you could see thick twists of white stars in the inky black night.

"I heard the sound of trickling water and noticed a star-shaped fountain in the middle of the room. Made of glistening white marble, it shone in the pale sunlight streaming in from above. We had stumbled into the most unlikely oasis in the Marrakech *medina*.

"Gladys perched herself on the edge of the fountain. Alexandra and Beatrice tentatively came through the front door and exclaimed, 'Oh!' at the same time.

"'Ladies,' Gladys declared knowingly. 'I'm

surprised at you. We're from New York City, after all. The Somerset girls, of all people, should know never to judge a room by the door leading into it. The more secret and hidden a place is, the better it is.'

"She took off her ladylike jacket and shook it, sending dust billowing into the air. It made a halo-like cloud around her in the sunlight. We were home at last."

Cornelia realized that the mint tea in her glass was now cold. She had been so wrapped up in Virginia's story that she hadn't taken a single sip.

Virginia stopped talking and stretched a little bit.

"Goodness, I hope I'm not boring you," she said to Cornelia. "Give me an audience, and I'll talk all after-noon." She reached down and scratched Mister Kin-yatta. The dog had curled himself into a ball and fallen asleep. His raspy snores sounded like little pig grunts.

"I'm not bored," said Cornelia. "Gladys was pretty brave. I would have been scared to go into that house."

"Yes, she was just like an elephant sometimes," said Virginia. "She would barge through any door in front of her, whether it was open, shut, locked, or nailed up."

Cornelia nodded. "Madame Desjardins is like that too, but not in a good way," she said. "She's always barg-ing into my room."

"Well," said Virginia thoughtfully, "have you considered

booby-trapping the door? Maybe some sort of lever system that would fling a pie in her direction? That might
work. Privacy is *very* important and it deserves to be
vigilantly protected."

Cornelia smiled and ducked her chin. She'd never
heard such an elegant adult use the word "booby-trap"
before.

"Do you have time for another story?" she asked
shyly. "I want to know what happens next."

"Oh, I suppose so," said Virginia. "If you insist."

"We settled very quickly into our disguised palace in
the *medina*. Alexandra and Beatrice were painters,
you see, and they set up their easels in the garden
behind the house and painted for days. I began
imagining on paper what sort of history had happened in our secret Moroccan manor. Gladys played
cards with Ahmed and Pierre and won all of their
money.

"When we took breaks from these various oc-
cupations, Pierre showed us around Marrakech
and the countryside. We went once to the ancient
market—called the *souk*—and to the hills around
the town and looked at the old mosques and lavish,
brightly colored Moroccan gardens."

"I like that word," said Cornelia with satisfaction.
"*Souk*. It's a pretty fancy way to say 'supermarket.'"

"Oh, you've got the wrong end of the stick, my dear,"

said Virginia. "*Souks* are *not* like sterile American supermarkets. In fact, they couldn't be more different. They are mazes of rickety stalls, teeming with people and filled with fish and cooking meats and huge barrels of pungent spices. Silver trays, copper teapots, and gold necklaces. Clucking chickens, hissing snakes, newborn lambs. Everything under the sun, even magic love potions! And it's all for sale. *Souks* are madhouses, I'm telling you."

"But Gladys was not satisfied with these occasional outings. Pierre began to cart her around everywhere with him, even on errands, but Gladys soon wore him out. She then made Ahmed take her all over Marrakech at all hours.

"One afternoon, Gladys and Ahmed were out for an especially long time. When they returned, Gladys joined Alexandra, Beatrice, and me for mint tea in the palm garden behind the house. As Gladys reached out for a glass, Alexandra looked at her sister's plump hand and shrieked.

"'Gladys Somerset! Did you get *tattoos*?' she cried, and recoiled.

"Gladys's fingers were covered in brown patterns, as if they'd been painted with a fine watercolor brush.

"'Oh, quit yapping. It's just temporary henna paint,' said Gladys as she reached for a honey pastry called *baklava.* 'This old woman in the *souk* painted me, and she did my feet too. In fact, she even painted a little anchor on my arm like the captain of the *Mauretania*. Apparently, Moroccan brides have it done before they get married.'

"'Gladys,' Alexandra said. 'Here's a news flash: you are *not* a Moroccan bride.' Beatrice and I giggled.

"Several days went by. One afternoon, it got extremely hot out and restlessness set in. Pierre and Ahmed had the day off and we had no one to show us around. We lazed in the house's cool marble tearoom and listlessly tried to think of something to do. Gladys threw herself about on a settee and sighed noisily behind a book.

"'Let's go to the *souk*,' she said at last as the settee creaked and groaned under her.

"'Are you kidding?' Beatrice answered. 'We'd get lost in about two seconds in that crazy jungle of shacks.'

"'You don't know your way around, but *I* do,' said Gladys. 'I know it like the back of my hand by now.'

"'Forget it,' said Alexandra, fanning herself with a palm frond.

"But once Gladys got a bee in her bonnet, she could be relentless. She pestered and cajoled and nudged us until finally we let her lead us like a tour guide into town.

"We had walked only a few dusty blocks from our house when we heard drums banging, followed by jangling bells and ladies trilling in high, shrill voices. All of the sudden, a parade of about fifty women rounded the corner and fanned out across the street, singing loudly and shaking instruments that looked like tambourines. They were clad in long bright dresses—sky blues, tangerine oranges, sunshine yellows—and veils covered their faces. They rumbled toward us like a thunderstorm.

"The sunlight shone brightest on a woman in the middle of the crowd. She wore the most ornate dress and veil and moved very slowly, her eyes cast down. Henna designs covered her delicate hands and feet, and we realized that this was a bridal procession. We clapped as they passed by, but the women took little notice of us. They disappeared around a dusty corner and the sound of their parade faded as they walked farther away. Then it was quiet again.

"Eventually Gladys led us triumphantly into the city's enormous main square, the Djemaa el-Fna. Surrounded on three sides by the *souk,* the middle of the square was filled with hundreds of people— buying things, selling things, shouting, running, mixing potions, charming snakes, skinning dead animals. All of them stopped and stared at us as we walked into the crowd. As you might have guessed, Cornelia, in 1949 in Morocco, you rarely saw four young American ladies strolling around on their own.

"'Stay together!' shouted Alexandra. She grabbed Beatrice's arm and I grabbed hers. Gladys barged through what seemed to us to be a wall of people. One man waited until we were about two feet away from him, and then he whipped the top off a basket at his feet. An angry cobra popped its head out and hissed at us. Beatrice blanched and we ran away, knocking into people behind us. The man gave a toothless laugh and clapped the top back down on the snake.

"'Everyone is pointing at us,' Beatrice cried. I let out a loud whoop as someone gave my bottom a hard pinch, and several men behind me laughed. I glared at them and scurried along next to my sisters. Soon Alexandra let out a yelp as the same thing happened to her.

"'All right, all right—I know how to put an end to this,' Gladys said.

"She plowed through the crowd toward a small stall selling traditional Moroccan women's clothing, and sorted through a pile of brightly colored clothes. *'Arbaha,'* she said to the owner of the stall, holding up four fingers and pulling out her coin purse.

"'Here are some disguises, so we blend in better,' Gladys told us, handing us each a dress. 'They're called *haiks.'*

"We ran to the edge of the square and slipped on our new outfits over our own clothes, looking sneakily around us.

"'What's this?' asked Alexandra, examining part of the garment.

"'A veiled hood to hide our faces,' said a muffled Gladys as she thrashed around inside her roomy dress.

"I tugged at my hood until I could see out through the veil. It was as hot as blazes inside. The only way I could tell the twins apart was by the colors of their dresses: Alexandra wore green and Beatrice wore red. Gladys looked like a big round orange under her *haik*. Now we could prowl around in the *souk* undetected."

"I would hate to wear a *haik*," Cornelia piped up. "It sounds completely incommodious." This meant "uncomfortable."

"Good word, Cornelia S.," complimented Virginia. "You're right—it wasn't the most pleasant thing in the world at first. But we Somersets have always loved theater and drama, and the *haik* was like a costume. Think about all of those heavy costumes that opera singers have to wear onstage all the time, the poor things. At least the *haik* was relatively light and roomy."

"Suddenly we heard the high, piercing shrieks of the bridal procession again. I turned around to have a look, but I stepped on my long dress and stumbled forward. Before I even knew what was happening, the women in the parade swept me up and carried me away with them. Confused and unsteady, I feared that the crowd would trample me into smithereens if I tripped again and fell down. I covered my ears to blot out the deafening sound of women singing and tambourines shaking.

"I caught sight of Beatrice's red dress and

grabbed her hand as we muddled along. 'Where are Alexandra and Gladys?' I shouted to her.

"'I'm behind you!' yelled Alexandra, and she tugged the back of my *haik*.

"Great cheers erupted from the crowds in the streets around the square as the bridal party pushed on. Then someone grabbed my arm and jerked me sideways out of the procession. I yanked my veil off and took several deep breaths of the dusty air. Alexandra, who had grabbed me, and Beatrice did the same.

"'Where's Gladys?' I gasped.

"'She must still be in the parade,' Beatrice said. 'I tried to grab her arm, but she was too far away for me to reach her.'

"'We can't lose her!' exclaimed Alexandra. 'Run after them!'

"So we began to chase the bridal parade as it wound into the maze of the *souk*. It finally halted in front of a big building like our secret house back in the *medina*. The ladies gave one last holler, and then all fifty of them filed into the house, with the bride in the middle of their crowd and Gladys mixed in someplace as well. Just as we reached the building, the last woman swept in and the doors closed with a thud. Beatrice tugged on one of them, but it stayed shut.

"'*Now* what are we going to do?' Beatrice wailed. 'Poor Gladys.' She paced back and forth in front of the building.

"'Let's be rational,' I said. 'This is a wedding, right? And at a wedding, there are guests. So, when guests start arriving, we'll slip in and pretend that we're invited. Hopefully, we'll find Gladys—if they haven't sent her off to jail yet for trespassing—and then we can scramble out of there.'

"Eventually the front doors opened and guests began to arrive. We decided that we'd look less suspicious if the room was full of people, so we lurked around in an alley along the side of the house for a while. Fortunately, the bride and groom appeared to know half of Marrakech, and the room filled up quickly.

"'Ready?' I asked, putting my veil back on. We tried to look very formal as we strolled up the front stairs of the house.

"An usher greeted us at the door. *'Ahlan wa sahlan,'* he said as he handed each of us a glass of mint tea. We nodded silently and walked into a large room filled with guests and waiters who walked about with trays of figs and almonds. At the far end of the room, the bride sat on a throne. She had changed into an even more elaborate dress, and a gold crown glistened on top of her veiled head.

"'It's about a thousand degrees in here,' Beatrice whispered in my ear. 'I bet the bride is absolutely dying under all of those layers.'

"She paused, and then said, 'You know what? Now that I'm getting a closer look, that bride seems pretty chubby all of the sudden. She didn't look that big on the street.'

"We edged closer to the throne to inspect her. I glanced at the astonishing henna patterns covering her hands and feet. Then I squinted at the left forearm of the bride and did a double take. Amidst the designs of leaves and stars, I saw a henna *anchor*! I almost passed out.

"'Beatrice and Alexandra,' I whispered. 'I've found Gladys.'

"Alexandra gasped and marched right up to the throne. 'Gladys Somerset—have you lost your mind?' she hissed, hoping that no one overheard. 'Who do you think you're fooling? We know that's you under there!'

"The 'bride' stirred a little under her costume. 'Help me, Alexandra,' Gladys wheezed from under the veil. 'This underdress is as tight as a boa constrictor. I can barely breathe. And for your information, this whole mess is *not* my fault.'

"'What do you mean, it isn't your fault? You're pretending to be the bride at someone else's wedding! Have you gone crazy? What happened to the real bride?' Alexandra huffed.

"'Well, on the way over here, I got smushed up next to her in the parade,' said Gladys from under the veil. 'Nice girl. Spoke good English. Anyway, she said that the groom was horrid and mean and that her parents were forcing her to marry him. But she's in love with a goat farmer from Casablanca and wants to marry him instead. So she begged me to switch places with her and I simply *had* to oblige. When we got here, we went to the bathroom and switched outfits, and she popped out the window.'

"Gladys shifted her bulk on the throne. 'It seemed like a good idea at the time, but now I think I'm in quite a pickle,' she added glumly. 'You and Beatrice and Virginia better do something pretty quickly, or I'm going to end up with a no-fun husband.'

"Alexandra strode back to me and Beatrice and told us what was going on. We sweated in our *haiks* as we tried to think of a solution.

"'We need to create a diversion before the ceremony starts,' Alexandra whispered, eyeing the groom as he walked around the room greeting guests. 'I have an idea. I'm going to create a big ruckus outside the front of the house. When the guests run to the front door to see what's happening, you push Gladys off that throne and out the back door.'

"She threaded her way through the crowd in the room and out the front door. Beatrice and I ambled nervously up to the throne and told Gladys to get ready to make a run for it.

"Several long minutes passed. Suddenly I heard the sound of something crashing into a herd of metal garbage cans in front of the building, and outside Alexandra shouted at the top of her lungs, 'Aaaaaaaaaaaah! My leg is broken! Oh, the agony! I'll never walk again! My life is ruined!'

"The music stopped immediately and the guests

and waiters scrambled to the front door to see what the fuss was about. Alexandra continued to wail outside.

"And then, as onlookers from the wedding hall rushed to her aid, she said, 'Oh, maybe it isn't broken after all. Heh, heh—what do you know? I can walk again! It's a *miracle*!' The jig was up.

"'*Now*, Gladys—before it's too late!' I whispered loudly.

"Gladys pitched forward off the throne as heavily as a marble statue. The three of us ran out of the room, down a hallway, and into another room at the back of the house. Gladys staggered around like a wounded rhinoceros. 'I've *got* to get out of this dress,' she moaned.

"'There's no back door!' I shouted. 'What are we going to do?'

"'We'll have to go out the window,' Gladys said as she threw her crown onto the ground and wrenched herself out of the dress. 'I *refuse* to go back in there and marry that man.'

"We squeezed ourselves out of the window and sprinted down the dirty alley behind the house, ripping off our *haiks* as we went. We must have run half a mile before stopping near a mule barn to catch our breath.

"It was only then that I realized that Gladys was clad only in her underwear. A donkey turned his head to look at us and began to bray, as if laughing with all of his might."

"Wait a minute," said Cornelia. "What did Alexandra crash into all of those cans?"

"She snatched a bicycle from a Moroccan kid down the street," Virginia replied. "And then she drove it into the garbage cans in front of the house to make as much noise as possible."

"Weren't the guests mad that she made such a cacophony?" Cornelia asked. "Cacophony" was a fancy word for "hubbub" or "racket."

"Sure, they were mad," said Virginia. "But in the end, they concluded that she was just another clueless American tourist. And then, when everyone realized that the bride was missing and got distracted, Alexandra grabbed the bicycle, limped it back to its owner as quickly as possible, and somehow made her way home through the *souk*. Without a map as well! As you can see, the Somersets were very resourceful girls."

Cornelia looked out the huge arched window and saw that it was getting late. Madame Desjardins would be expecting her soon for dinner. She didn't want to leave, but on the other hand, she didn't want to overstay her welcome.

"I should probably go," she said reluctantly, and slid off the bed. "It's getting late."

"Oh, what a shame," said Virginia coyly. "I was just getting to the best story. I *suppose* it can wait for some other time."

Cornelia stopped in her tracks. "What sort of story?" she asked.

"A scary one this time," said Virginia soberly. "But if you're late for something, then go ahead." She sighed and extended her hand out in front of her, admiring her ruby rings, and then slyly glanced at Cornelia.

"I suppose I have time for just one more," said Cornelia, looking meaningfully at her empty spot on the daybed.

"Oh, good," said Virginia. "I always love telling an old-fashioned, shivery ghost tale."

"The day started out innocently enough. The summertime sun beat down on Marrakech, and the four of us took refuge in a cool sitting room in our hidden house. The twins lay on opposite ends of a long couch and looked like damp mirror images of each other. Gladys sat near the window with her nose jammed in a guidebook about Morocco. I ran ice cubes across my forehead and counted the minutes until sunset.

"'It's so scorching hot today that when I tried to paint outside this morning, the tubes melted,' Beatrice told us for the third time that day.

"'Hmmm,' said Gladys, not really paying attention.

"'Everything feels so drowsy,' Beatrice complained. 'Not even the dust is stirring outside.'

"'Mmm-hmmm,' murmured Gladys, turning

another page. Alexandra just nodded and fanned herself.

"Gladys snapped her book shut. 'It's always hotter when you're just lying around,' she said. 'Let's take a trip. I've found someplace wonderful for us to go.'

"'Where, a beach?' I asked hopefully. 'An ancient shaded date grove?'

"'No—Meknes,' Gladys answered.

"'*Where?*' I asked. 'What's that?'

"'Meknes is a city, Virginia,' Gladys said impatiently. 'I just learned about it. Listen to this.' She read aloud from her book:

"'About three hundred years ago, a cruel sultan named Moulay Ismail came into power. He had dozens of wives, and then he decided that in addition to those, he wanted to marry a French princess. But the French king at the time refused to give up one of his daughters, and this made the sultan cranky. So he decided to take revenge on the king. At that time, the French city of Versailles was one of the most spectacular cities in the world. So Moulay Ismail decided that he would embarrass the French king by building a city more spectacular than Versailles.'

"'And did he?' asked Alexandra.

"'Well,' said Gladys, 'he made tens of thousands of workers and slaves work on the city for years and years. They built palaces and miles of walls and huge *souks*. But this book says that that ole Moulay didn't even live to see it finished. And to top it all off, when he died, two clocks were hung near the entrance to his tomb. Gifts from the French king, which he'd sent instead of a French princess. That's what I call poetic justice. Let's go for the day. I'll go tell Ahmed and Pierre.' And she stomped out of the room.

"A mere thirty minutes later, Alexandra, Beatrice, and I found ourselves wedged with Gladys into one of the cars along with a picnic basket, a camera, binoculars, and the guidebook. Ahmed and Pierre sat in the front seat, arguing over the maps and directions. My sisters and I wore our hats and white gloves to protect us from the harsh afternoon Moroccan sun. Only a few hardy souls meandered around on the streets of Marrakech as we drove out of the city.

"We drove for hours before we reached the desert-like outskirts of Meknes. And let me tell you, Cornelia, it was no Versailles. Three centuries after Moulay Ismail was gone, his city was more like an old ruins. We parked our car near the town's ramshackly old *souk*, mostly stalls filled with barrels of olives.

"'Come, come,' Pierre said as we got out. 'I will take you to one of the palaces.' He flicked open one of the maps of the town center and traced over it with his finger. 'Ah. Here is one. Follow me.'

"The four of us followed him in a neat little line.

Ahmed trailed behind, greeting the owners of the *souk* stalls as we went.

"Soon we saw a huge fortress surrounded by a vast wall that seemed as tall as a skyscraper in New York City. The sun looked huge and pink as it sank toward the horizon, and our shadows made long, dramatic shapes on the ground. No other tourists loitered outside the wall with cameras, and no ticket sellers or tour guides approached us. We were all alone and the palace appeared empty.

"Pierre shrugged. 'Why don't you go in and sneak a quick look,' he said. 'No one will notice. We will wait for you here and be the lookouts. You come out when it gets dark, which is soon.' He glanced at the sky and lit a cigarette. Ahmed did the same.

"'Are you sure?' asked Alexandra. 'What happens if we get discovered inside without a ticket?'

"'They will think that you are a spy and then they hang you,' Pierre said. He and Ahmed laughed. 'Or the ghost of Moulay Ismail will come and make all four of you marry him.' They laughed again.

"Gladys had heard enough. She whipped out her guidebook and walked through the front entrance, a huge arch lined with beautiful patterned tiles. As usual, the other Somerset sisters followed her.

"We walked through a huge outdoor courtyard, and then into a long cloistered hallway. The palace had been abandoned many years ago, and now it was deserted and almost completely silent, except for our footsteps and whispers. The light faded outside and the rooms and courtyards along the hallway grew grayer. All of the windows were glassless, so once in a while we could hear the melancholy evening wind blowing the dust around outside.

"'Look at the ceiling,' Beatrice said softly, as though she were in a church. 'That must have taken someone many years to do.'

"The dome above our heads looked like a puzzle made of millions of assorted tiny colored tiles—all kinds of stars, shapes, and patterns. The ceiling and walls of the next room were covered in the same way. In the floor of each room lay an empty marble fountain, dry as a bone for generations. We must have walked through a hundred rooms like that, all of them echoing with eerie, vacant grandeur.

"Finally, we wandered into a huge banquet hall.

"'Look at that!' said Gladys, startling all of us. She pointed to a curious ancient wooden door in the back wall. Brass door rings as big as dinner plates hung on it, and an enormous rusty bolt ran across the middle. Gladys walked up to the door and examined her guidebook.

"'There should be a big courtyard with an orange grove behind this door,' she concluded, squinting at the page in the dusky light.

"'We should go back,' Alexandra said. 'What if we get locked into this place by accident? They must close it at night. I mean, it might be empty, but it's still a palace, after all.' Beatrice and I agreed and turned around to leave.

"'You're all acting like a bunch of old ladies,'

Gladys said with a scowl. 'Did we come all this way for nothing? I want to see the orchard. It'll only take a few minutes.'

"She heaved the bolt on the door upward and it creaked open with a rusty groan. Gladys wiped her filthy hands on her skirt and leaned into the door with her shoulder. It grudgingly opened a crack.

"'Virginia,' she said imploringly. 'Help me open this.' We pushed together and finally it opened far enough for us to squeeze through.

"'*There's* the problem,' Gladys said, pointing to a big rock on the other side of the door. She bent down and shoved the heavy stone backward. The door swung freely on its hinges now, and Beatrice and Alexandra followed us into the twilit courtyard. We could see the first stars coming out in the sky above us, but no moon.

"Tall walls sealed in the yard, which was filled with long rows of small, gnarled orange trees. In the sunshine, you could have seen the trees' bright green leaves and plump oranges, but at night, the trees looked metallic and sinister. Even though it had been a hundred degrees earlier in the day, a sudden chill swept over us.

"Beatrice shivered. 'They meant business when they made that outer wall,' she said, nodding toward the back wall of the garden. 'It's so tall and it must be twenty feet thick—probably impossible to climb.'

"'I read that Sultan Moulay Ismail was infamous for his brutality to the slaves who built these walls and palaces,' Gladys explained grimly. 'When they died from being overworked, the sultan had their bodies thrown into the walls as building material.'

"'Gladys Somerset!' Alexandra shrieked. 'You'd better be making that up!'

"'No, I'm not!' Gladys protested. 'It says it right here, on page 257.'

"'I'm going back,' I said. The very idea of a body-filled wall nauseated me.

"Without warning, the door behind us slammed shut in the wind. I ran to it and gave it a yank, only to hear the ominous clang of the rusty lever falling down into place on the other side of the door, locking us in the courtyard.

"Our only hope of getting out rested with Ahmed and Pierre, who hopefully would come looking for us now that it was getting dark. We decided that we couldn't shout over the wall to them, since we probably weren't supposed to be in the palace in the first place and didn't want to attract attention. So we just sat there, huddled on the edge of a stone terrace, waiting and staring queasily at the far wall of the courtyard.

"'I wonder if it's true about the wall,' Beatrice said.

"'If it is,' Gladys said, 'then I bet that this is one of the most haunted places in Morocco.'

"The trees swayed gloomily in another gust of wind. The hairs on my arms stood on end and I got goose bumps all over.

"'I wonder what a three-hundred-year-old ghost

looks like,' said Gladys. 'And if it would like Americans. You never know in these parts.'

"'Be quiet, Gladys,' we all said together.

"'I guess this is a bad time to tell you that the sultan would also cut off the heads of his stable hands once in a while,' Gladys added. 'I think the stable is just over that side wall there.'

"'Be *quiet,* Gladys!' we shouted."

Before she could help herself, Cornelia let out a little yelp.

"What's the matter?" asked Virginia, startled.

"I got goose bumps," said Cornelia. "About the ghost wall." All of the hair on her arms was standing up.

"The atmosphere was portentous, I assure you," said Virginia dramatically. This word meant "showing a sign of evil or calamity to come."

Cornelia understood perfectly and hugged a pillow to her stomach. "Go on," she urged.

"Well, by this time, darkness completely shrouded the courtyard and the stone terrace felt like ice underneath my bottom. I put my head down on my knees and wished that we were anyplace in the world besides this eerie graveyard.

"Just then, a long light flickered across the terrace, coming from a slit between the door and the doorframe.

"'That's got to be Pierre and Ahmed!' Beatrice exclaimed.

"A thin line of orange light illuminated her face as she leaned in to peer through the crack. Gladys was about to shout out to them when Beatrice looked back at us and made a quick slashing motion across her throat with her finger. We froze.

"'It's *not* Ahmed and Pierre,' she hissed. 'There're about five men, and they must be Moroccan soldiers. They do *not* look happy.' She tiptoed over to us. 'What if they think that we were trespassing and they're looking for us—to arrest us?'

"Gladys padded up to the crack and peeked through. 'Now there are a lot of them,' she whispered. 'They're definitely not soldiers. They look like servants from the old days, and they're filling the room with torches. Ladies, these are *ghosts*. I'm sure of it.'

"'Ghosts?' I whispered. 'I don't believe it!' Alexandra's and Beatrice's faces went pale.

"'You'd believe it if you saw what I'm looking at,' Gladys answered ominously. She watched for another minute. 'Now they're bringing in long tables and setting them up. Here come the chairs. And candles . . . and they are scattering *rose petals* everywhere. Can you believe it? What on earth is going on?'

"The voices of dozens of men came from inside as they set up furniture in the fire-lit room. I nudged Gladys aside to peek into the room. Men wearing long white traditional robes brought musical instruments into the room and set up a small orchestra in the corner of the room. They looked pretty solid for ghosts, but I'd heard stories about real-looking phantoms before.

"'What are we going to do?' I whispered to my sisters. We each took turns watching the preparations in the hall. Suddenly someone shouted something in Arabic inside and then the orchestra began to play. It was Gladys's turn at the door, and she reached out and grabbed my arm.

"'It seems that some very important men just came in and sat at one of the tables,' she whispered. 'And one of them is dressed like an ancient sultan. He's quite fat, if I do say so myself. I can't see the other ones.'

"I imagined Sultan Moulay Ismail presiding over a lavish feast three hundred years ago in that very room, attended by terrified servants. Was history being repeated before our very eyes?

"'I want to look,' whispered Beatrice, giving Gladys a prod.

"Gladys waved her away. 'Now they're bringing out huge silver platters of food,' she told us. 'Who ever thought that you could smell ghost food? But it looks good, whatever it is.'

"'Gladys, it's my turn!' whispered Beatrice indignantly.

"Gladys didn't budge. Beatrice stamped her foot and gave Gladys a little shove. Gladys stepped backward, but she had forgotten about the sullen rock that had held the door shut. She stumbled backward over it, lost her balance, and fell down noisily, letting out a resounding squawk.

"The music stopped inside and footsteps thundered toward the door, followed by the sound of the rusty lever being pushed up. The door flew open, bathing us in light from inside the hall. Several Moroccan men stared out at us in great surprise. Gladys lay on the terrace with her skirt up around her waist. One of the men suppressed a laugh and rushed out to help her up. The others reached out and took us by the arms, pushing us into the banquet room. Everyone in the room stared at us. Gladys was right—the feast looked and smelled delicious, and my stomach ignored my fright and rumbled loudly.

"The man who Gladys described as the sultan sat at a table. At his side sat several men wearing modern business suits, making this the most peculiar of ancient supernatural gatherings. One of them let out a gasp and stood up when he saw us.

"'What on earth!' he exclaimed in English. 'The Somerset girls! I absolutely don't believe it! What in heaven's name are you *doing* here?'

"'Mr. Plitt?' Alexandra croaked. 'What are *you* doing here?'"

"Who?" shouted Cornelia, very excited by this time.

"Mr. Edwin A. Plitt," said Virginia matter-of-factly, as if Mr. Plitt's appearance at this time made all the sense in the world. "He was a great friend of our father's from New York. He was very short and as round and brown as a walnut, with a neatly cropped mustache shaped like an umbrella over his mouth."

"My sisters and I gaped in shock at Mr. Plitt, who proclaimed, 'I am currently the American ambassador to Morocco, ladies. In fact, I saw your parents at a dinner party in New York about a month ago, and they told me that you were in the country. I promised them that I'd personally check in on you, and here you are! And you look . . . um . . . splendid!' Which, as you can imagine, Cornelia, we did not.

"'But what in Sam Hill were you doing lurking about in the courtyard?' he asked, and said hastily to a young man standing next to him, 'Please explain to His Highness the sultan and his guards not to be alarmed, and that these ladies are in fine standing in New York.' The translator relayed this message in Arabic to the sultan, who appeared to be very amused. Plump and relaxed as an old pillow, he still managed to look very regal.

"'We were just admiring the orange trees in the moonlight,' Beatrice offered ridiculously.

"'I see,' said the ambassador dubiously. 'It is indeed a fine palace. His Highness Sultan Mohammed V has been kind enough to host me for dinner in this majestic but tormented shrine to Moroccan history. Your Highness, may I present the Ladies

Somerset: Alexandra, Beatrice, Gladys, and Virginia. Such as they are.'

"As we bowed to the sultan, he snapped his fingers, and suddenly four men carried another table and four chairs into the room.

"The translator turned to us and said, 'His Highness Sultan Mohammed V requests your presence at the feast which you see before you. He says that you seem like fine women of adventurous character.'

"And with that, we found ourselves seated at an extravagant banquet with the royal ruler of Morocco. The music started again, and the men turned their attention to the food.

"'I am absolutely mortified,' Alexandra said in a low voice. 'I can't believe that we met the sultan of Morocco when we look like this, and that we barged in on a royal dinner for the ambassador! Our parents will kill us when they hear about this.'

"'Barged in?' cried Gladys, whose hat was still tilted sideways on her head from her fall. 'We did not. We were invited to dine.' A waiter laid a beautiful lamb *tagine* and pear in front of us, followed by many other dishes of delicious Moroccan food. 'And just in time,' continued Gladys, shaking a napkin out and placing it on her dusty lap. 'I'm famished.'"

Mister Kinyatta woke up and looked around sleepily. He stretched and shook his huge ears. A delicious smell wafted in from the kitchen down the hallway.

"Mmmm," Virginia said. "Incidentally, that's what

lamb *tagine* smells like. It's one of my favorite Moroccan dishes. Patel must have gotten inspired by my storytelling."

Cornelia's heart skipped a beat. "Is it dinnertime already?" she exclaimed. "I have to go."

"Thank you for spending the afternoon with me, Cornelia S.," said Virginia, reclining on the silk pillows again. "You are a wonderful listener, and that's just as important as being a good storyteller." She thought for a minute. "Well, *almost* as important anyway."

"I'm not a good storyteller, though," said Cornelia. "I don't have anyone to tell stories to, and anyway, if I did, no one understands my long words. I'm a linguistic recluse." By this, she meant that she was a person who withdraws from the world and into words.

Virginia looked at Cornelia quizzically. "Well, words have many uses, as you will learn. I like to share them with as many people as possible." She yawned. "And don't forget that *I* understand your long words. They will be our secret code."

Cornelia nodded, thrilled to have a new partner in crime. She thanked Virginia and ran home to the chill of her apartment next door.

Chapter Five

The Souk in Hell's Kitchen

❋

Several days after Cornelia's visit with Virginia, Lucy came home from her vacation. She strode into the apartment and heaped her luggage in a little mountain near the front door. Cornelia ran out of her room and down the stairs to greet her mother.

"Hello, darling," Lucy said, and gave Cornelia a big showy kiss on her forehead. Lucy was very brown from the Moroccan sun, and Cornelia felt like a pallid, melted snowflake next to her. "Look how tan your mama is! Isn't it lovely?"

"Yes, very," said Cornelia.

Madame Desjardins bustled out of the kitchen into the hallway. "*Bonjour*, Madame!" she said. "Welcome home."

"*Bonjour*, Dominique," Lucy said, walking down the stark white hallway to the study. Dominique was Madame Desjardins's first name. "The apartment looks perfect, as usual. Oh! Before I forget—can you bring my luggage in to be repaired this week? One of the cases got damaged on the flight back. I'll need it back as soon as possible."

"Ohhh," said Madame Desjardins tentatively. "Madame must have forgotten that this is my week off." There was an uncomfortable silence. "I am going to my family's house in France tomorrow morning," she added apologetically, wringing her hands.

"Ah," Lucy said finally. "You're right. I had forgotten. When will you be back? Don't forget that I'm leaving for France myself at the end of the week, for that concert in Paris."

"I am back in time for your trip, Madame, do not worry," Madame Desjardins said. Both women then looked at Cornelia, who stood there in the hallway as quiet and still as a teacup.

Lucy cleared her throat. "So, you and I will have a lovely week together then, won't we, darling?" she said to her daughter. Cornelia nodded.

The next afternoon, Lucy picked Cornelia up from school in a taxi.

"Darling, I have to bring you on an errand with me," Lucy said from behind a huge pair of sunglasses. "I know it's boring, but Ingrid is cleaning at home. She's in such a fierce mood that I'm afraid that she'll vacuum you up if I leave you there."

The taxi smelled like Lucy's perfume, and Cornelia snuggled into the seat next to her mother. It was very cold outside, and their breath clouded up the back windows.

"Where are we going?" asked Cornelia, praying that it wouldn't be a sit-in-a-restaurant-for-three-hours type of errand.

"Ugh—to see Melvin Horowitz, my accountant," Lucy replied unenthusiastically. "Ugh, ugh, ugh."

Normally, the prospect of going to see an accountant would be enough to send any eleven-year-old into a tantrum, or at least a dour sulk. But Cornelia liked old Melvin, who was the most peculiar sort of person. First of all, Melvin worked only for artists, people like Lucy. Secondly, he didn't have an office. In fact, they never went to see him in the same place twice. And the places where they did meet up with him were very odd for an accountant. For example, once he had set up a workspace in the old stables at Central Park. Another time, he worked from a comic-book factory on the Lower East Side.

"I hate offices," he told Cornelia once. "Hate 'em. All of those buzzing fluorescent lights. You might as well be working in a graveyard."

Cornelia, who had not had a lot of experience with offices herself, somehow understood and appreciated his resourcefulness.

Today, the taxi pulled up in a neighborhood on the West Side of Manhattan called Hell's Kitchen, an area once infamous for its gangs and riots and squalor. Lucy and Cornelia got out of their taxi in front of a rickety building that looked like a dirty old factory. Cornelia looked up at it warily, and imagined that the Somerset sisters must have felt the same way when they first reached their secret house in Marrakech.

"Melvin's in *there*?" she asked.

Lucy lowered her sunglasses to the tip of her nose and then pushed them back up. "That's what he told me on the phone this morning," she said. "Who knows what else is in there with him. Have courage, Cornelia."

They rang the front bell and the door promptly buzzed open for them. Cornelia remembered what

Gladys had said about never knowing what to expect on the other side of doors in New York City. When she and Lucy walked through this particular door, they entered an enormous yarn warehouse. The dingy ceilings loomed thirty feet above their heads, and rows of high shelves, crammed with big spools of yarn in every imaginable color, filled the room. Dim lightbulbs hung on wires suspended from the ceiling.

"Come in, come in, lickety-split," Melvin called from some faraway, unseen corner. "I'm in the back."

They walked up one aisle and down another, and then up yet another one before they found him. A rabbity little man, Melvin had pointy ears and glasses that swung dangerously on a chain around his neck. His nearly bald head glistened in the dreary light, except for one piece of hair that he had swirled elaborately around his head.

"Oooh, call the press! They're here at last!" he shouted when he saw Lucy and Cornelia. He leaped up from behind his desk, made from a big door on top of two big wooden crates. "What do you think of my new headquarters?" he asked. "Wait! I'll roll out the red carpet."

He bounded over to a nearby shelf stuffed with yarn and snatched up a maroon spool. Holding the end of the string, he threw the spool along the floor toward Lucy, unraveling a long line of dark red yarn between the two of them. Lucy laughed, walked over to Melvin, and gave him a kiss hello on his cheek.

"Hello, Melvin darling," she said. She gestured toward Cornelia. "Do you remember my daughter? Madame Desjardins, our housekeeper, is away this week. I hope you don't mind."

"And hello, Miss Cornelia Street," said Melvin, looking down at her. "Look at those big hands. You'll be a pianist soon too, just like your mother. Here," he added, handing her a wad of licorice. "It's all yours. I bought it for myself, but it practically ripped out every tooth in my head. You look like you got strong teeth."

Cornelia disliked licorice. "I'll defenestrate it right away," she said. The word "defenestrate" meant "to throw something out a window."

"That's my girl," said Melvin. And then he and Lucy sat down at the door-desk and started to muddle through piles of paperwork and receipts. Cornelia wandered up and down the aisles, looking at the thousands of colored spools. When the licorice got sticky in her hands, she surreptitiously stuffed it under a spool of thick puce-colored yarn.

"Oh, no!" said Melvin to Lucy, several aisles away. "You can't deduct Louis Vuitton suitcases as a travel expense. Nice try, you minx. By the way, Cornelia is starting to look less like her daddy and more like you all the time."

Cornelia stopped in her tracks, and she practically popped her eardrums straining to hear the rest of the conversation.

"Yes, she is," Lucy said. "But she has his mouth." Cornelia heard Lucy light a cigarette.

"You ever see him?" Melvin asked.

"No," said Lucy. "And I don't read his reviews or listen to his CDs either. I'm just glad that he lives in Europe, so I don't have to keep running into him around town."

"That's a shame, just a shame," Melvin said. "And it would be even more of a shame if Cornelia didn't play that piano of yours, being the daughter of two famous piano players like you and Leonard."

"I don't want to force her," Lucy said. "If she wants to play, I'll get her lessons. But whenever I ask her, she says she never wants to learn."

"Don't let hands like that go to waste," advised Melvin. It was quiet for a minute while they worked.

"You ever gonna take that kid with you when you go on a trip?" he asked. "She looks like she could get out more."

"Oh, be quiet, Melvin," Lucy said. "She's too young. And she wouldn't be interested in going to my concerts. I spent all of my teenage years traveling around and playing in concerts, and look what happened to me."

"Harrumph," said Melvin, looking unconvinced and

shuffling some papers around. Then something caught his attention. "Oh, give me a break. Now, what is that, Lucy? You wanna write off this Moroccan retreat as a medical expense?"

Cornelia stopped listening. Numbness spread to her hands and feet. She knew everything that Lucy had told Melvin already, but any mention of her father always gave Cornelia an unpleasant jolt.

She tried to distract herself from thinking about the situation by walking around the warehouse again. She pretended that she was in a *souk*, and that people and donkeys and spices and rugs filled the warehouse. When she reached the aisle of green yarns, she imagined that she was sitting down for some mint tea with the Somerset sisters. In the red aisle, she pretended that they were buying more *haiks*. When Cornelia got down to the far end of the warehouse, in the brown aisle, she imagined that they were visiting the henna lady. She got completely lost in her own thoughts and didn't even notice Melvin and Lucy standing at the end of the corridor, looking at her.

"Cornelia," Lucy said. "Who were you just talking to?"

Cornelia snapped to attention. "I was just pretending," she said, her cheeks burning with embarrassment.

"Thank you, Melvin darling," Lucy said. "We've staved off prison and poverty for another year, I think."

Melvin helped her into her coat. "Of course we did," he said, still looking curiously at Cornelia. Then his phone rang back at his door-desk and he galloped off to answer it, hooting good-bye to Lucy and Cornelia as he went.

"What were you pretending, Cornelia?" Lucy glanced down at her daughter as they got into another taxi.

"That I was at the *souk*," Cornelia said. "Buying a *haik,* or going to see the henna lady. That place just reminded me of how it all might look."

Lucy looked at Cornelia in surprise. "Where did you learn those words? Did I tell you about them?"

A wave of regret and protectiveness washed over Cornelia. Suddenly she realized that she didn't want Lucy to know about her new friend. She wanted to keep the world next door and Virginia's stories to herself. What if Virginia and Lucy met and, even worse, became friends? Then Cornelia would stop being Cornelia in Virginia's eyes; she would just be Lucy Englehart's daughter, as usual.

"I've been learning all about it in school," Cornelia said casually, and looked out the window.

Lucy continued to gaze at Cornelia, clearly skeptical. "What else have you learned about?"

"All sorts of things," answered Cornelia, feeling safe behind the shield of her lie. "About sultans and mint tea and Moroccan weddings and old palaces with walls that have dead bodies in them."

"Oh," Lucy said after a minute. "Well. I never learned such interesting things at school." They were silent for a block or two, and then Lucy continued, "Morocco is a wonderful place. When you're older, you can go there yourself and see." She stretched her hands out on her lap. "Now we have to scramble home so your mama can practice the piano. The noose of the Steinway tightens, and Rachmaninoff must be practiced." She sighed.

"What?" asked Cornelia.

"What I mean, darling," Lucy said, "is that I have another performance in Paris next week. At a very important concert hall, the Salle Pleyel." She smiled and smoothed Cornelia's hair. "Maybe they'll teach you about Paris next in school."

Or maybe you can tell me something about it, or take me with you for once, Cornelia thought ruefully. *But I won't hold my breath.*

The trip to the yarn *souk* in Hell's Kitchen was really the only time Cornelia spent with her mother that week. Lucy spent the days and nights thundering away at her piano, getting ready for her concert. Ingrid came every afternoon that week to straighten up, and ordered dinner to be delivered to the apartment each night before she went home. When the food arrived, Lucy abandoned the *Bête Noire* and emerged from the music room, with thick curls of cigarette smoke wafting out the door after her. She and Cornelia ate sitting on stools in the kitchen. Lucy's tan grew paler and her mood darker, as it always did before a big performance.

When Madame Desjardins came back on Sunday, a sense of normalcy returned to the apartment, for which Cornelia was surprisingly grateful. Lucy left for Paris the next day before Cornelia got home from school.

Cornelia was secretly glad about Madame Desjardins's return for another reason as well: the housekeeper was simply easier to fool than Lucy. That afternoon, Cornelia devised a little plan on her walk home from school. When Madame Desjardins opened the front door, Cornelia marched in and put her bag down.

"Madame Desjardins," she declared. "Lauren Brannigan asked me to go over to her house to work on a science project together. Can I go? She lives just up the street, remember?"

"Oh, *oui,*" said Madame Desjardins. "Yes, the little girl with that horrible, nosy mother. When I see that woman on the street, she always talks to me forever about Madame Lucille. Are you sure you want to go?"

"I have to," Cornelia said. "It's a school project."

"You can walk up by yourself? So I can stay here and cook dinner for us?" Madame Desjardins asked hopefully.

"I *always* walk up there on my own," said Cornelia, delighted that her scheme had worked so far.

Of course, the second the door shut behind her, Cornelia walked straight up the hallway to Virginia's door and rang the doorbell.

"Oh, hello, Cornelia-ji," said Patel, opening the door. "Come in, come in." Cornelia kicked off her shoes in the foyer. "I have something to show you," Patel told her. "You will like it."

They walked down the long corridor, through the velvet curtains at the far end, and into the Moroccan forest room.

"Oh!" exclaimed Cornelia when she saw the surprise. She ran to the center of the room, where the star-shaped marble fountain had just been installed. Twenty-five big, fat bright orange goldfish circled around in the bubbling water.

"Look!" said Patel, pointing to a fish filter in the back of the fountain. "Your idea. You are a very smart girl. And no new pipes in the floor, so everyone is happy." The sound of gurgling water soothed Cornelia so much that she wanted to climb up onto the sumptuous daybed for a nap.

"Virginia is in her French drawing room," Patel said. "Come with me." They went back through the curtains and walked up to a closed door. "Go visit with her, and I will bring you something to eat," he promised.

Cornelia knocked on the door. *"Entrez-vous!"* called out Virginia from inside. "Come in!"

"It's me, Cornelia," said Cornelia, opening the door.

Today, Virginia sat in an enormous, overstuffed silk chair by the window, peering outside through a set of binoculars. Mister Kinyatta slept curled up on a matching footstool at her feet. He opened one eye when Cornelia came in, then closed it, snoring again in no time.

"Oh, hello, Cornelia S.! Come sit down." Virginia adjusted the focus on the binoculars and looked through them again. "Did Patel show you the fountain? I am so happy with it." And then she squinted through the glasses and said, "Oh, my!" She leaned forward and pressed the binoculars against the window.

"Are you watching the boats?" Cornelia guessed. She craned her neck to see if there was any excitement on the river.

"Heavens, no. I'm spying on people," Virginia responded unrepentantly. "This is one of the ways I get ideas for my stories, through spying." She looked at Cornelia. "All you need to see is a little bit of someone's life, and you can imagine the rest. I'm sort of shopping for a story right now." She squinted into the binoculars again. "Oh, my goodness!"

"What's happening? Can I look?" Cornelia asked.

"Um, I don't think that's a good idea." Virginia fumbled with the binoculars, suddenly embarrassed. "Anyway, I think I need to have these fixed. They're a little cloudy."

She pushed the binoculars under the skirt of the chair, leaned back, and smiled. She was wearing her gold filament scarf over her head today, and a long pearl-colored dress with a fluffy fur collar. "How are you, Cornelia? I gather that your mother has been home. Patel and I heard a little bit of her playing through the wall."

"Yes," Cornelia said, sinking sullenly into a chair opposite Virginia. "She was practicing a lot for her concert in Paris. She left again this morning."

"Oh, _j'adore_ Paris! And speaking of the City of Light, did you notice my French drawing room?" asked Virginia.

Cornelia had not, but now she looked around. Thick silk the color of a robin's egg covered the walls. Both the ceiling and floor appeared to have been made of gold, as did all of the furniture. A gigantic white marble fireplace mantel, big as a walk-in closet, was carved into the far wall. A heavy gilded mirror hung above it, suspended by string as thick and strong as piano wires. The regal formality of the room suddenly made Cornelia want to curtsy, but since she didn't know how, she sat up very straight instead.

"I modeled it after a drawing room of the French queen named Marie Antoinette," Virginia said. "Beastly woman, but she had good taste in drawing rooms."

"It's very pretty," Cornelia admitted. "But it makes me feel like I have to really mind my manners all of a sudden." But then she slouched again and looked at her hands.

"That's because it's French," said Virginia mysteriously. "I write my letters in this room. And I have my breakfast and read newspapers here. And spy, of course."

They were quiet for a moment, and then Virginia asked, "Is everything all right today, Cornelia?"

Cornelia slid down in her chair and focused on her kneecaps jutting out from under her skirt. "What are you supposed to do when you miss somebody?" she asked vaguely.

"Well, I miss my sisters terribly," Virginia answered thoughtfully, drumming her fingers quietly on the padded arm of her chair. "So I try to do things that remind me of them. And I surround myself with things that remind me of them. And of course, I tell stories about them to other people." She looked at Cornelia gently. "I'm sure that you miss your mother when she's away giving concerts."

"I guess so," said Cornelia. "Sometimes. Although it's nice to have time to myself as well. But is it possible to miss someone you've never met?"

"Absolutely!" Virginia declared. "Half of the world is

in love with someone they've never met, and never will meet. And each of those poor souls misses their mystery person terribly."

"At least you were together with your sisters all the time," Cornelia said, tears welling in her eyes. "I don't have any family, except for my mother."

"Cornelia," Virginia said softly. "I'm sure that you get lonely sometimes without brothers or sisters—or your father. When someone's missing from your life, it can be terrible. I think that's one of the reasons I became a writer, actually. You can't wish a person into existence in real life, but you can on paper, and those characters take on a life of their own. You can make them behave in any way that you want, and you can spend as much or as little time with them as you like.

"But," she continued, "in any case, it's important that you don't spend too much time dwelling on the people who are absent, for that is a *very* slippery slope. More than anything, you have to appreciate the people who really are around you. Too many people realize at the end of their lives that they've taken for granted those who really love them."

Cornelia stared at a gold writing desk across the room. "I like being around you, and Patel. And Mister Kinyatta." A tear streaked down along her nose. "I wish that I had sisters like yours."

Virginia smiled. "Those sisters were a mixed blessing, I assure you. I can't tell you how many times I
wished that I were an only child, when Beatrice stole my
toys or Alexandra bossed me around or Gladys got me
into trouble. The grass is *always* greener on the other
side."

Just then, Patel came in with a tray.

"Don't cry, Cornelia," Virginia said, rising up from
her chair to see the top of the tray. "It's actually sunny
out today, and we're going to eat some delicious treats.
One of my favorite lady writers, Isak Dinesen, used to
eat only oysters and drink champagne, which is on my
menu this afternoon. That's how I like to honor her
memory," she said jauntily.

Patel set the tray down on a little table near Virginia.
"For Cornelia-ji, I have brought a *chocolat chaud* and a
tarte aux pommes," he said.

Cornelia wiped her cheeks and looked at the cup of
steaming hot chocolate and the lovely apple tart that
Patel had brought for her. She smiled at him and
straightened up. He handed her a linen napkin and left
the room.

"*Dhanyavaad,* Patel," Virginia called after him.
"That means 'Thank you' in Hindi," she told Cornelia.
"Mmmmm, this looks good. Gladys was always partial
to a good *tarte aux pommes.*

"Look over there," she added, pointing to another black-and-white framed photograph on the writing desk. "That's a picture of the Somerset sisters in Paris, where we went after Morocco." She teased an oyster out of its shell with a tiny gold fork.

Cornelia got up and looked at the picture. This time, the Somerset ladies stood near a sunlit river in a city with a huge cathedral looming in the background. Just like in their Morocco photograph, they all wore nearly matching hats. Cornelia looked down around their ankles and counted four little dogs that looked just like Mister Kinyatta. Beatrice held their leashes and was the only one in the photo scowling.

"Why does Beatrice have all of those dogs?" Cornelia asked.

"That's interesting that you can tell Beatrice from Alexandra," said Virginia with a raised eyebrow. "Very few people ever could. Until they opened their mouths, that is."

"The difference is obvious," said Cornelia knowledgeably. "Alexandra looks more magisterial." In less polite terms, this meant that Alexandra looked bossier than the others.

Virginia laughed. "That's true. And regarding the dogs: we acquired them through a big blunder. But if the mistake hadn't been made, I wouldn't have Mister Kinyatta here. One of those dogs is his great-great-great-grandfather, and the others are his great-great-great-uncles. Or something like that."

Cornelia went back to her chair and took a bite of her *tarte aux pommes*. "I wonder what my mother is doing in Paris right now," she said. "Do you have any good stories about when you were there with your sisters?"

Virginia smiled again. "What a silly question," she said, reaching for another oyster. "Of course I do."

Chapter Six

Paris, 1950

"The summer sun in Morocco was so punishing that we decided to go north. We packed up and said good-bye to Pierre, Ahmed, and our secret palace in the *medina*. Then we took a train to Casablanca, boarded a ship, and in no time at all, we were in France.

"Alexandra, Beatrice, Gladys, and I lived in another hidden home in Paris. Our mother had arranged for us to live in a vine-covered house in Paris's oldest and most beautiful square, the Place des Vosges. The edges of the square were made up of matching grand houses that reminded me of pink cakes with white frosting edges. In the middle of the square sat a perfect open park with hedgelike trees and fountains. Royalty and aristocrats and artists had lived in the noble houses for centuries, but I loved the square because many famous writers had lived there. The twins loved it because it was perfectly symmetrical, each side exactly matching the opposite side—rather like Alexandra and Beatrice themselves. And Gladys loved it because all sorts of bloody sword duels had taken place there hundreds of years before.

"Our hidden house had no exact address, and when we first arrived in Paris in a taxi, we drove around and around the Place des Vosges looking for it. Finally, we spotted a big wooden arched door without a house number in one of the pink buildings. It reminded me of the door in the sultan's banquet room in Meknes.

"'Here we go again,' Gladys said, and leaped out of the taxi. She pressed her thumb into a buzzer next to the door.

"After a moment or two, a small older woman opened the door. She wore little glasses and looked as neat as a present.

"'*Bonjour,* Mademoiselle Somerset,' the woman said. She was holding a photo of us that our mother had sent to her. She glanced at it for a second, and then looked back at Gladys, eyeing her up and down. 'You are Gladys,' she said. '*Je m'appelle Madame Laloux.* I am Madame Laloux. *Entrez-vous, s'il vous plaît.* Please do come in.'

"Madame Laloux was the owner and *gouvernante,* or housekeeper, and she lived on the fourth floor."

"Oh, no," interrupted Cornelia. The word "house-keeper" always raised a red flag for her. "I bet she chased you around the house a lot, like Madame Desjardins does to me."

"Well, that was the idea, I guess," said Virginia. "Our mother wanted someone to keep an eye on us, after hearing of our adventure in Morocco from the ambassador in Morocco. But Madame Laloux was a strange old woman who came downstairs only to clean the house and serve us breakfast, lunch, tea, and dinner. It was an ideal arrangement. Three thousand miles away, our mother thought that we had a chaperone, and we really had all the freedom in the world. And just wait until you hear about the house itself."

"The four of us followed Madame Laloux through the heavy wooden door, which led into a tall arched tunnel. A pretty garden spread out on the other side of the tunnel and in front of our vine-covered house. Tall and quite narrow, the building bent a little bit this way, and then back in the other direction. Its eleven window boxes overflowed with crimson flowers, and petals blew like parade confetti in the breeze.

"Inside, the house had four floors of drawing rooms, living rooms, parlors, writing rooms, libraries, and bedrooms. All of the rooms had special couches called *chaises longues* and silk-covered walls and old ticking clocks and marble fireplaces and ancient heavy wooden beams in the ceilings.

"The next morning, after a good night of sleep in deep feather beds, we ate croissants and cheese for breakfast in a quaint parlor on the first floor. Beatrice read from a French newspaper and tortured us as she tried to pronounce the words.

"'That sounds terrible,' said Gladys, her mouth full. 'Why don't you take lessons?'

"'My French is *parme*,' Beatrice said defensively. 'Which means "perfect." And the rest of you barely even know the French words for "yes" and "no," so you should all be grateful that I'm here.'

"'Actually, I think that you meant to say *parfait*,' said Alexandra with a teasing smile. 'Which means "perfect." *Parme* means "violet." And I'm afraid, dear Beatrice, that your French is neither *parme* nor *parfait*.'

"At that moment, Madame Laloux walked into the room, taking tidy little steps. 'A *télégramme* from your *mère*,' she said, placing a white envelope on the middle of the breakfast table and hurrying out again.

"Beatrice grabbed the envelope and tore it open. She chewed a little bite of croissant as she read it over. 'Oh, how dull,' she said, tossing it back on the table. 'Mom wants us to call a special shop and order her some Limoges china vases—four of them—and ship them to her in New York right away.'

"'Well, Beatrice,' said Gladys. 'Since you speak

parme French and we don't speak a word of it, I guess that fun task will fall to you.'

"Beatrice glared at her and reached for her French dictionary, which was on the sunny window-sill behind her. 'I know how to say "china" in French already, but I'm just making sure,' she announced. She thumbed through the book. 'Aha! It is just as I thought. You say *chine.*'

"With her nose in the air, she marched out of the breakfast parlor to the telephone room down the hall. We heard her saying '*chine, chine*' over and over to herself, trying to make herself remember the word. Gladys winked at Alexandra and me.

"We sipped our cups of tea while Beatrice placed the order. Warm morning sunshine filled the room. A few minutes later, Beatrice raised her voice on the phone down the hallway.

"'*Non, non—chien! Chien!*' she shouted. '*Quatre!*' which means 'four.' This went on for quite some time. Finally, she strolled back to the break-fast parlor and sat down.

"'That took forever,' Beatrice complained. 'I had a terrible, scratchy phone connection and the shop woman on the other end couldn't understand me. She kept telling me that they didn't have any china vases—"*Chien? Non!*" Finally, she sighed and said she'd see what she could do.'

"'Oh, quit carping,' said Gladys. 'Let's go explore.'

"And out we went. We walked all around the Place des Vosges and through the narrow streets of our neighborhood, or *arrondissement,* and down to the Seine River to look at the long rows of fine white houses on the riverbanks. Once in a while, we would come across a whole street of houses that had been reduced to rubble."

Cornelia interrupted again. "How did the houses get knocked down?" she asked. "Was there an earthquake or something?"

"No," said Virginia. "Paris had been hard-hit during World War II, and a lot of houses had been destroyed. Many people died. Sometimes Gladys would point out holes that had been made by bullets in the sides of buildings. It was a very disturbing but fascinating time to be in Paris."

"We went to a brightly lit, noisy café for lunch and pretended to understand the menu. Beatrice ordered four plates of *escargots,* promising us that this meant 'steak.' Imagine our surprise when four dishes of garlicky snails came to the table instead.

"Several hours later, we ambled back to our hidden house. When we knocked on the big wooden door to the hidden garden, Madame Laloux's footsteps pitter-pattered quickly up to the door, as if she were an overwound toy. She flung the door open.

"'Mademoiselle Somerset!' Madame Laloux cried, pointing a bony finger at Beatrice. '*Non, non,*

non! A big mistake has been made! Come with me.'
And she scuttled down the path to the vine-covered
house. Dumbfounded, we trundled after her.

"'*Regardez!*' Madame Laloux exclaimed, fling-
ing open the door to the downstairs drawing room.
The four of us tried to cram ourselves into the narrow doorway to examine the mysterious crisis. I
was stuck behind Gladys and couldn't see into the
room.

"'What on earth!' shrieked Beatrice. 'Where did
they come from?'

"Alexandra let out an 'Oh!' and Gladys snickered. I stood on my tiptoes and finally saw the cause
of the commotion: three little French bulldogs lay
on the couches and one more was curled up on the
hearth of the room's fireplace. They leaped up and
sixteen paws scrambled toward us.

"'When your mother writes to me, she says "my
four daughters come to stay with you"—she does
not say four *chiens! Mon Dieu!*' squealed Madame
Laloux. 'And then a woman from a shop comes
today and says that Mademoiselle Beatrice Somerset has ordered four *chiens* for right away!'

"One of the dogs leaped back up onto an exquis-
ite silk settee and pawed the cushion a little bit.

"'Beatrice, you *idiote,*' said Alexandra with an
amused undertone in her voice. 'I know what happened. You must have used the wrong word in your
phone order this morning. Instead of saying *chine,*
you probably said *chien.* Which, as you know,

means "dog"! Someplace in between the breakfast parlor and the telephone room, you got the words mixed up. "And, *anyway* . . . *chine* wasn't even the right word to begin with! *Chine* means 'China,' the country, not china dishes, Miss Know-It-All. And now we have no vases for our mother, and four French bulldogs to take care of.'

"One of the dogs began running in crazy circles around the room, exciting the others.

"'Well,' said Gladys, reaching down to pick one of them up. 'I know whose room they'll be sleeping in.' She gave a sideways glance toward Beatrice.

"'Ohhhh,' moaned Beatrice, clapping her hand to her forehead. 'What am I going to do? I'll have to call that storekeeper back and tell her to come and get them!'"

"Gladys lifted the dog to eye level and nudged its nose with her own. The dog rewarded her with a lick. "Too late. I've already bonded with this one. The real question is this,' she said. 'Who gets to write to our mother and tell her that we've adopted four new Somerset babies?' She smirked naughtily. 'We could address the note to "Grandmother Somerset." I predict a panicked telegram back within the day.'

"Madame Laloux glared at her. *'Folle à lier,'* she said under her breath, and she clicked huffily away to the kitchen.

"I looked this phrase up later. It meant 'Mad as a hatter.'"

Cornelia leaped up and kneeled in front of the footstool where Mister Kinyatta lay asleep. She scratched his head between his big bat ears. Still asleep, he rolled over on his back so she could tickle his tummy.

"Thank goodness that Beatrice got the dogs and not the vases," Cornelia said, petting the dog's white tuxedo chest. "Otherwise, who knows where Mister Kinyatta would be living now?"

"He'd be in a Parisian apartment with some old French lady instead of an old American one," replied Virginia. "And his name would be something like Jacques or Pascal."

"I think the name Mister Kinyatta is infinitely preferable," said Cornelia.

"I'm partial to it myself," said Virginia, nudging the beast with her toe. "I named him after a friend from India, but I'll tell you about that later. I can only concentrate on one country at a time."

"So, did you and your sisters get into any more trouble in Paris?" asked Cornelia.

"Now, Cornelia," said Virginia. "I think you know the answer to that question already."

"Several weeks went by, and Madame Laloux eventually forgave Beatrice. We moved all of the good furniture out of the front drawing room, which became the dogs' room, and we brought cushions home from a flea market for their beds. Beatrice named the dogs Un, Deux, Trois, and Quatre—One, Two, Three, and Four. I added 'Monsieur' to the beginning of each of those names. Since then, all of our dogs have been Mister this or Mister that. We bought yellow leather leashes for them, and they—not Madame Laloux—became our constant chaperones.

"One afternoon, we put on our hats and took a stroll down to an area called Montparnasse. The trip took a long time and my feet ached with exhaustion by the time we got there. Gladys steered us to a famous old café named La Closerie des Lilas and melodramatically collapsed onto a chair at a table on the outdoor terrace. Beatrice struggled through the jumble of tables as Messieurs Un, Deux, Trois, and Quatre dragged her in four different directions. They settled down after our waiter emerged from the kitchen with huge beef bones on a silver tray for them.

"We had just ordered some *moules* to eat when a screech erupted from a nearby table. Two women leaped up from their table and one of their chairs fell over behind them. 'Un rat! Un rat!' they shrieked.

"Everyone around us jumped up. At that moment, I saw a blur of gray fur and pink tail dart past our table. All four of the dogs tried to bound after it, but Beatrice grasped their leashes tightly.

"'Gah!' she cried, straining to hold on to them. 'They're so strong! They look so little, but they're like trucks!'

"Monsieur Trois gave an extremely spirited pull on his leash and yanked it out of Beatrice's hand. He shot through the tables and chairs and ran off the terrace after the rat.

"We practically turned our table over in our rush to chase after him. People in the streets shook their heads as we tore past them, shouting the dog's name.

"Monsieur Trois took a right on Boulevard Raspail and scurried up the street. I was sure that he would run in front of a speeding car. He was going so fast that his hind legs practically touched his nose with each bound. The rat must have turned into the entrance of a building, for suddenly Monsieur Trois skidded sideways to a stop and clambered into the building after the rodent. We ran in after them, not noticing a sign above the front door proclaiming:

LES CATACOMBES

"We stumbled into an entrance room to some sort of museum, just in time to see Monsieur Trois run down a spiral staircase that descended through the floor. We started after him when a bad-tempered old woman sitting behind a desk let out a piercing screech, followed by a chastising torrent of French.

"'*Mon chien! Mon chien!*' shouted Beatrice at her, struggling to control Messieurs Un, Deux, and

Quatre as she pointed to the staircase. The woman stood up, yelled, and shook her head. She reminded me of the witch in *Hansel and Gretel*.

"'She wants us to *pay* her to go down there,' Beatrice told us frantically. We shook our pocketbooks upside down until a few coins plinked onto the floor, and before the woman could protest, we picked up the dogs and trampled down the staircase after Monsieur Trois. Gladys deftly snatched a brochure on the way down.

"The staircase wound on and on, delving deep underground. The air in the stairwell began to smell musty and odd. Monsieur Trois barked someplace in the space below us. Hundreds of steps later, we finally reached the bottom of the staircase and found ourselves in a dimly lit room with several doors leading to different hallways. Now I knew how Alice in *Alice in Wonderland* must have felt after she fell down through the rabbit hole.

"'Which way did he go?' wailed Beatrice. 'He could be anywhere. We'd better split up and follow him.'

"'No way,' Alexandra said, peering at the pictures in the brochure Gladys had swiped. 'I'm not going anywhere in here by myself, so you can just come up with a different plan.'

"She pointed to a sign above one of the doors. 'Do you see *that*?' she cried. It read:

ARRÊTE! C'EST ICI L'EMPIRE DE LA MORT."

"What does that mean?" Cornelia asked, suddenly fearful.

Virginia paused ominously. "Are you sure that you want to know?"

Cornelia nodded.

"It means 'Stop! This is the Empire of Death,'" said Virginia. "Now, *this* is where the story gets good."

"We fell silent when we figured out what the sign said. The dogs sniffed the floor and backed away from the entrances.

"'I've read about this place,' said Beatrice. 'It's called the Catacombs, and it's a ghastly underground maze of bones that were moved here from a cemetery hundreds of years ago.'

"Alexandra covered her face with her hands. 'Why,' she said from behind her fingers, 'can we not have just one normal tourist experience? Just one? A nice stroll and a nice little lunch? Why do we always have to end up in a bizarre graveyard or wedding or sultan's feast?'

"A Monsieur Trois yap echoed down one of the corridors.

"'We're wasting time! He'll get lost forever—or hurt,' shouted Beatrice. Messieurs Un, Deux, and Quatre panted around our ankles and strained toward one of the corridors. 'He must be down this way,' she said. The dogs pulled toward the passageway under the grisly sign.

"Several heavy flashlights lay in a pile on one side of the room, probably used by workers who needed to navigate the maze for one reason or another. Alexandra grabbed one and switched it on, casting a dim beam of light onto the path in front of us. We barreled down the dark corridor, calling for Monsieur Trois, but he always seemed to be just around the next corner. The shadowy passage went on and on, and turned first left, then right, and left again.

"Then Alexandra stopped abruptly and shone the flashlight along the walls. We saw thousands of what looked like blanched sticks, and then I realized that they were actually bones. It was worse than Sultan Moulay Ismail's wall. My stomach surged, and even Gladys looked repulsed.

"Messieurs Un, Deux, and Quatre barked like crazy when they saw the bones. We scooped them up and carried them down the sinister corridor. Some of the workers who had built the labyrinth must have been perverse and grim artists, arranging hundreds of the bones into designs in the walls. At one point, we actually walked past a wall that featured nine grinning skulls shaping the outline of a heart.

"Suddenly the dogs smelled something and started barking. A dog yelped in the dark ahead of us. We ran toward the noise, and Alexandra shone the beam of the flashlight on a dark shape in the passage. Two shifty little black eyes glittered in the light. It was Monsieur Trois, gnawing on a smelly old shoe. Gladys swooped down and picked him up.

"'You *bête*,' she said. 'Didn't get your rat, did you? And now we're stuck in this maze of bones, when we should be drinking *chocolat chaud* at La Closerie des Lilas. *Merci*, Monsieur Trois.' He licked her and looked longingly at the shoe.

"'Where did *that* old thing come from?' Alexandra asked, kicking it down the hallway.

"'Well, we don't know who else might be down here,' said Gladys. 'This place was used during the war as the headquarters of resistance fighters. Maybe the shoe belonged to one of them. Or maybe some strange, horrible person still lives down here, limping around in the shadows and eating rats for dinner.'

"'That's it—I'm getting out of here,' I said, and spun around.

"We tried to retrace our steps back to the winding staircase, but all of the hideous corridors looked so similar that we got confused. I feared that we would have the same bad luck that we did in Meknes and get locked into this necropolis.

"'Shush,' whispered Beatrice, slowing for a minute. 'Did you hear something just then?'

"We stopped and listened. Something scuffled in the dark behind us. The hairs on my arms rose as I imagined a ghoulish stalker lurking in the dark, and I could hear my own heart pounding in fear. At the same time, I realized that Alexandra's flashlight was getting dimmer as its batteries ran low.

"'Just keep going!' hissed Gladys. 'We have to get back to that staircase before the flashlight dies!'

"We started to run. My eyes smarted from the murky dust that we kicked up from the floor.

"'I can still hear that noise!' exclaimed Alexandra. The beam of the flashlight bounced around the floor in front of us as she hurried along. 'Someone is definitely following us!'

"We ran even faster, but we seemed to be getting nowhere, as though we were in a bad dream. The sound of footsteps behind us, clear as bells now, speeded up as well. Finally, we saw a dim light ahead of us: we had found the room with the spiral staircase!

"'There it is!' shouted Beatrice. 'Run as fast as you can!'

"The dreaded footsteps behind us quickened, along with huffing and puffing as the person tried to catch up with us.

"Just as we got to the staircase, something crashed down behind me. I spun around and saw Beatrice sprawled out across the floor. She had tripped on the pile of flashlights. Monsieur Quatre leaped out of her arms and ran back into the dark passageway behind us. Then a shriek came from the corridor, along with a great deal of barking and snarling.

"Suddenly a figure staggered into the room, with

Monsieur Quatre nipping at its ankles. To our shock, we realized that it was the old woman from upstairs! Had we *really* been pursued like fugitives through the so-called Empire of Death by an eighty-year-old ticket-taker? We gaped at each other in humiliated disbelief. Alexandra dove for Monsieur Quatre as he sank his teeth into the woman's skirt and tugged as hard as he could.

"'*C'est une brute! C'est une brute!*' the old woman yelled, kicking her stumpy foot in his direction. The dog growled at her even after Alexandra snatched him up.

"'*You're* the brute—not him!' I yelled at the woman as I grabbed Beatrice's arm and pulled her up from the floor. 'Why are you chasing us?'

"The old woman began another vicious flood of French and stamped her foot at us.

"'What's she saying?' Gladys asked a now dirty Beatrice.

"The woman took out a handful of coins and shook her fist at us. Beatrice grimaced as she tried to understand the woman. Then she began to laugh. 'I think she's saying that we didn't give her enough money upstairs,' Beatrice said. 'And that we have to pay her now or she'll call the police.'

"Alexandra opened her purse, fished out some more coins, and handed them to the woman, who counted them with relish. The amount must have satisfied her, for all of the sudden, she smiled generously and waved her arm gracefully toward the staircase. She even patted Beatrice neatly on the shoulder and said something into her ear. We scrambled up the stairs to street level and ran out of the building. The fresh evening air had never smelled so good.

"'What did that witchy old thing say to you on the way out?' I asked Beatrice.

"Beatrice smirked and cleared her throat. 'She said that she hoped that we enjoyed our tour, and that we're welcome back anytime,' she announced. 'And now we'd better go back and pay our bill at La Closerie des Lilas, or we'll have our waiter from this afternoon chasing us down the street as well.'"

Cornelia ran her finger around the rim of her cup to get every last bit of *chocolat chaud.* "I can't believe that the old woman actually wanted you to pay her to see a bunch of bones," she said. "How preposterously morbid."

"It is gruesome, I agree," said Virginia, shielding her eyes from the late-afternoon sun streaming in. "Apparently, these days, Les Catacombes are a big tourist attraction, although I preferred to spend my time at La Closerie. I heard that the famous author Ernest Hemingway wrote one of my favorite novels, *The Sun Also Rises,* on that same terrace."

"I know who he is," Cornelia said. "My mother gave me a thesaurus that once belonged to him."

Virginia raised her eyebrows. "Now that's an enviable gift," she said. "Maybe it will bring you luck. I hung around the Closerie café for hours, hoping that some of Hemingway's luck and influence would rub off on me."

"And did it?" asked Cornelia.

"No, it did not," said Virginia matter-of-factly. "It's true that I've written tons of clever stories over the years, yet I'm still waiting to write my great novel. Fortunately, however, I've just had the most wonderful idea for one, and right in the nick of time."

"That's good—what will the book be about?" Cornelia asked, wondering what Virginia meant by "in the nick of time."

"Well, I'm afraid that I can't tell you," answered Virginia. "It will have to be a surprise. Writers and artists are a moody lot, and we never tell or show *anyone* what we're working on until it's done."

Cornelia sank back into her chair, disappointed. She wanted to know about Virginia's new story, but she, of all people, certainly had to respect the importance of privacy.

"Then can you at least tell me one more story about France as a consolation?" she asked.

"Well, since we're already on the subject of *artistes* in Paris," said Virginia, "I'll tell you a story about our encounter with Pablo Picasso, one of the most famous artists in world history. It's a favorite tale of mine."

"It was springtime in Paris, which everyone knows is the prettiest time of the year there. Pale pink and white flowers covered the trees and sunshine warmed the streets. I spent much of my time writing on a little balcony on the front of our vine-covered house. Gladys stomped around Paris, investigating all the battle sites of the French Revolution, a civil war that happened one hundred fifty years earlier. Alexandra and Beatrice set up their easels all over town and painted street scenes.

"Everything was peaceful and lovely—until one afternoon when Alexandra and Beatrice burst into the tea parlor after visiting a gallery on the Left Bank. They had clearly been quarreling.

"Gladys, who was filling her plate with pastries, looked at them without much concern. 'What disturbeth the twins Somerset?' she asked, wiping her fingers on the napkin in her lap.

"'Nothing, except that Alexandra is trying to steal the limelight away from me once again,' said Beatrice peevishly as she sat down.

"'*I'm* stealing the limelight from *you*?' Alexandra cried. 'Ha! I'd say it was the other way around.'

"This went on for a few noisy minutes until Gladys pounded her fist on the table, making the éclairs fly up into the air. Only then did we get an explanation.

"'Well,' said Alexandra, daintily placing a napkin on her lap. 'After lunch, the two of us went to a gallery to see the new Picasso paintings. While we were there, the most interesting man came up and started talking to me about the art on the walls.'

"'I think you *meant* to say that he came up to talk to *me!*' exclaimed Beatrice.

"'Have a tart, Beatrice,' said Alexandra. 'You're clearly so hungry that you can't remember things straight. *Anyway,* this man walked around the whole gallery with us and only an hour later did he reveal that *he* was Picasso! Then I told him that I'm an artist too, and he *immediately* offered to give me lessons at his studio.'

"'No, he offered to give *me* lessons!' shouted Beatrice. 'And then Alexandra asked him if she could have lessons as well. I can never do anything on my own. It can never be just Beatrice Somerset by herself. Alexandra Somerset always has to be right there at my side, tagging along.'

"Alexandra's face grew red. 'Beatrice! What a lie! You know very well that the opposite thing happened! Monsieur Picasso asked *me* to be his pupil— and you're just jealous, as usual.'

"Gladys winced as the exchange grew shriller and louder. 'Enough of this!' she bellowed. 'Who cares who got invited first? You're both going now, so you might as well share your paints and the taxi fare and be happy about it.' She glared at both of them. 'All of your bickering is ruining the taste of these pastries.'

"The next day, Alexandra and Beatrice threw all of their paints into a satchel and climbed into a taxi to Picasso's studio, where they began their lessons.

Relations between the two of them, however, remained chilly. They were rarely cross with each other, but when they were, it was like being near a slow-building thunderstorm with intermittent angry cloudbursts.

"Then, several weeks later, there was another Picasso-related quarrel at the dinner table. The twins had just returned home from a day at the studio, toting canvases and brushes. Gray and blue and green paint still caked their fingernails.

"We ate a lovely *coq au vin* in silence. Gladys attempted to cheer everyone by telling us a story about a terrible queen whose head had gotten lopped off during the French Revolution. I listened appreciatively, but the twins still glared at each other over the table.

"'So, listen to what Pablo said to me today,' Beatrice said. 'He told me that I'm the most beautiful woman in all of Paris.'

"Alexandra let her fork fall to the plate with a clatter. 'Oh, *really,*' she said. 'Fancy that. He just happened to tell me the same thing yesterday.'

"You can imagine how that went over with Beatrice. Within seconds, they started shouting at each other again. The dogs, begging for food under the table, began to look concerned. Monsieur Quatre came and huddled next to my leg.

"'Knock it off—both of you!' Gladys finally hollered. 'Who cares what that man told either of you? He probably says that to the fishmonger's wife! And he's only had about a hundred wives and mistresses. Do you have to ruin every meal fighting about him? And anyway, you look exactly alike, so I don't even see what all the fuss is about.' "

Cornelia grimaced. "This story is making me glad that I don't have sisters," she said. "For the first time in my life."

"I *told* you that they were a mixed blessing," said Virginia. "Now you know what I mean." And she continued.

"The next day, the twins went off to their lessons as usual, still fuming at each other. By late afternoon, they were back at the house. They filed into the tea parlor and sat down. Their moods had changed. Alexandra looked as calm as a nun, and Beatrice's face was flushed with triumphant defiance.

"'Ladies, it will soon be decided,' Beatrice announced as she poured milk into her tea.

"'What will?' asked Gladys suspiciously.

"'Who is the more beautiful of the two of us,' said Alexandra haughtily. 'And which one of us Pablo prefers.'

"'Oh, no,' moaned Gladys. 'What have you done?'

"'Nothing,' insisted Alexandra, exuding innocence. 'I simply marched into the studio today and asked him to make up his mind. Or rather, that he tell Beatrice the truth: that he thinks I am the prettier one.'

"'Now, this is what is going to happen,' Beatrice

said, ignoring Alexandra's last statement. 'He told us about a Greek myth in which three powerful goddesses got into a fight over who was the most beautiful. A man named Paris—ironic, huh?—was called in to decide among the three. And so Pablo says that this will be like a modern version of that contest.'

"'So,' Alexandra interrupted, 'over the next three weeks, he'll officially decide who's prettier. Once he's made the decision, he'll paint a huge, important portrait of the winner. And then he'll throw an enormous party in his studio and invite everyone in Paris to the unveiling of the painting.'

"'I'm going to spend this week with him in his studio, being sketched,' said Beatrice, 'and Alexandra's going next week. The week after that, he will paint the victor's portrait.'

"Gladys and I looked at each other in dismay. We could see already that the next three weeks were going to be horrible.

"So, that week Beatrice traipsed to Picasso's studio each day to be studied and sketched by him. She came home each night looking very confident. Seven days passed, and then Alexandra went to the studio instead. The twins made a great show of being civil to each other during that time, for each was sure that she'd win. Gladys couldn't stand the tension and spent most of her time out of the house, at the jazz clubs in an area called St. Germain des Prés. I barely came inside from my balcony, except to eat and sleep.

"On the fifteenth day, Picasso called the twins to

his studio and told them that he had made his decision. He scheduled the party at which the winner's painting would be revealed for a week later.

"Invitations went out to all of the artists, aristocrats, journalists, musicians, actors, and politicians in Paris, requesting their presence at the conclusion of this unusual contest. Newspapers and magazines wrote about it, and people in cafés on the riverbanks speculated about who would win and even placed bets. Before long, the twins became celebrities in Paris, and everyone wanted to know which one Picasso would choose.

"The big night finally arrived. Gladys and I reluctantly agreed to go with the twins to the party. Beatrice came downstairs dressed in a big silver ball gown, with flowers in her hair. Alexandra followed her five minutes later, wearing a black ball gown and a diamond tiara. Not wanting to draw attention to myself, I donned a plain green gown and wore no jewels. And I don't know what on earth Gladys was wearing, but she looked like she was clad in a burlap sack of some sort.

"'*Très chic,* isn't it?' she whispered to me proudly, smoothing down the coarse fabric.

"'May the best lady win,' said Beatrice, sticking her hand out in front of her. Alexandra shook it elegantly, and we all climbed into a waiting taxi.

"When we arrived at Picasso's large studio, quite a crowd had gathered outside. Flashbulbs popped as photographers took pictures of the twins getting out of the car. Reporters shouted to us to answer a few questions. They went absolutely crazy when Gladys lurched out of the car. She happily posed for the photographers, and then clomped inside after us.

"'They loved me,' she said breathlessly.

"Important, glamorous people from all over the city packed the studio, and waiters milled through the crowd carrying trays laden with champagne glasses. I spotted Picasso for the first time, deeply absorbed in conversation with three pretty, doting actresses. A wreath of white hair wrapped above his ears and around the back of his head, which was shining bald on top. He had very intense dark eyes and a broad, strong nose. While many of the men in the room wore tuxedos, Picasso wore a black-and-white-striped shirt, making him look like an escaped prisoner. He smoked continuously and seemed to be enjoying the whole affair immensely.

"On the far wall of the studio hung the painting. Hidden by a huge red velvet drape, it nearly covered the whole wall. Once the room was overflowing with people, Picasso stood on a chair in front of the shrouded painting. He put two fingers in his mouth and whistled loudly. The crowd hushed and everyone faced him, and flashbulbs popped as he talked.

"'Ladies and gentlemen,' he began. 'Because our guests of honor tonight are American, I will give this speech mostly in English. All of you know why you are here. I have made my decision, but before I reveal it to you, I will introduce you to my two muses.

First, *je vous présente* Miss Alexandra Somerset, who is a Hera *moderne*.'

"Alexandra walked up through the crowd toward the artist. Hera was the name of one of the goddesses in the fabled Greek contest. As the queen of the gods, Hera was very handsome and arrogant. The crowd cheered as Alexandra took her place next to Picasso. With her tiara, she looked very regal herself.

"'And now, *je vous présente* Miss Beatrice Somerset, who is our Athena *forte*,' the artist shouted.

"Athena, the warrior goddess, had been another contestant. Accordingly, the word *forte* means 'strong.' More applause erupted from the crowd, and Beatrice's silver dress glinted like armor in the spotlight.

"'And now, it is time to show you my choice,' said Picasso as he leaped off the chair and strode up to the painting. Everyone in the crowd held their breath. I grasped Gladys's hand nervously. The moment had come at last.

"Picasso grabbed the velvet and tore it from the painting. *'Voilà!'* he shouted.

"Suddenly both Alexandra and Beatrice let out a terrible shriek at the same time. The crowd surged forward to inspect the result, and Gladys and I stumbled ahead with the mob. Everyone erupted into uproarious laughter when they saw the painting.

"'What's going on here?' Gladys yelled to me, scowling. She barreled through the crowd to the front of the room and roughly pushed several photographers aside. We stood in front of Picasso's work at last—and gasped.

"It was *horrible*! The painting showed a woman's body with two heads that faced each other and appeared to be screaming bloody murder. Farther down, the creature scratched at its body with clawed hands. The title underneath the painting read:

La Bête avec Deux Têtes

Or, in English, 'The Two-Headed Beast.'

"Picasso stood proudly in front of his work, clearly reveling in the commotion he had caused. The photographers feverishly snapped pictures of Alexandra and Beatrice as they reacted to the painting.

"'*You're* the beast, not *us*!' shouted Beatrice, pointing at Picasso. She faced Alexandra. 'That horrible man! We can't let him get away with this, Alexandra!'

"'Absolutely not!' Alexandra yelled, enraged. The twins snatched up the hems of their dresses and plowed through the crowd to the far side of the studio. When they reemerged at the front of the room again, they carried huge buckets of paint in their hands.

"'Now!' Beatrice cried, and with all of their might, they threw paint all over Picasso and the painting. The crowd cheered more wildly than ever and the photographers went crazy again. Beatrice spotted Gladys and me amidst all of the faces, and she and Alexandra ran toward us.

"'Let's get out of here!' she shouted. The four of us pushed through the crowd out of the studio, past the journalists and photographers outside, and ran down the street.

"A full, heavy moon lit the night sky, and we decided to walk home along the Seine River. The twins looked at each other's ruined dresses and started laughing.

"'I secretly thought that he was a bad artist all along,' said Alexandra. 'He hardly got a detail of either of our faces right, even after all of that sketching.'

"'That painting looked like it was done by a five-year-old,' Beatrice snorted. 'He should have been taking lessons from *us*.'

"'And by the way,' Alexandra said to Beatrice, looking down at her sister's paint-spattered ball gown, 'our mother would be so proud of your outfit tonight. It would make every debutante in New York green with envy.'

"They laughed together, linked arms, and walked on ahead of Gladys and me.

"And that was the end of the art lessons with Picasso."

Cornelia wanted to stand up and cheer. "I can't believe that Alexandra and Beatrice had the temerity to throw paint on him like that," she said. "Temerity" meant "boldness" or "audaciousness."

"I was astounded too," said Virginia. "But Gladys and I were very impressed by their resourcefulness. The Somerset sisters really *did* know how to create a spectacle."

"Well, that man deserved it," said Cornelia, her spirits much higher than when she'd come into Virginia's apartment earlier that day.

"Do you want to hear an amusing postscript to that story?" Virginia asked. "Years later, I read a magazine interview with Picasso, and he talked at length about the contest. He said that it was a shame that the painting had been ruined, for he thought that it was one of the best he'd ever done.

"And the funny thing is, it would probably be worth tens of millions of dollars today if he had simply put away his paints and cleaned up before having company over."

Chapter Seven

The Howling Dog

One afternoon several weeks later, Cornelia came home from school to find an unpleasant surprise in her apartment. When Madame Desjardins opened the front door for Cornelia, she immediately put her finger to her lips and whispered, "Shhhhhh! Your mother is practicing with Madame von Harding. Why don't you run up to your room for a little while, and I'll bring you a snack."

Cornelia scowled. Nina von Harding was Lucy's best friend and an imperious opera singer. Every few months, she came to the apartment and Lucy played the piano while Nina sang. She had such a powerful voice that once she had sung a china vase off a table in the living room, like a shrill siren luring a sailor to his death. Disgruntled neighbors always slipped notes under the door after practice sessions with Nina.

After the piano itself, Nina was Cornelia's gravest enemy. They had never liked each other. When Cornelia was little, around four or five years old, she liked to sit at the top of the staircase and howl like a coyote whenever Nina sang in the music room below. Once, after Cornelia had let out a particularly wrenching caterwaul, Nina threw open the doors to the music room and marched to the bottom of the staircase. She pointed a long, bony finger up at Cornelia.

"You," she said accusingly, "are a terrible child. Just *awful.*"

And then she burst into tears. Cornelia giggled. Lucy ran out and collected Nina. She steered the weeping singer back into the music room, shooting Cornelia a boy-are-you-in-trouble look before she closed the doors. Cornelia had always considered it a quiet victory, and her private nickname for the lady was "The Howling Dog."

Today, however, Cornelia secretly didn't mind being shuttled up to her room, for she had a package in her coat pocket that she wanted to open right away. When she had walked into the lobby of the building a few minutes earlier, Walter had stopped her.

"Come over 'ere, lassie," he had said to Cornelia

sternly. "A small parcel came in the post for you." And he opened the closet door behind the front desk.

Cornelia had been genuinely astonished. Who would have sent something to her? Lucy was here in New York, and in any case, she was not in the habit of sending gifts to Cornelia from faraway locations.

"Cheerio—'ere it is," said Walter, his voice muffled from inside the closet. He emerged holding a small cardboard box, which was indeed addressed to a Miss Cornelia S. Englehart. The return address was a bookstore. Walter had looked at her inquisitively as she turned the mystery package every which way.

"So, Miss Cornelia, d'you have a boyfriend who's sendin' you presents, then?" he had asked her jokingly.

"Don't be ludicrous," Cornelia had said, blushing as she tucked her prize into her big coat pocket and walked quickly to the elevators. "Ludicrous" was Cornelia's showy word for "ridiculous."

Now Madame Desjardins reached for the collar of Cornelia's coat, ready to help her take it off. "Oh," she said. "It must be raining out still."

Cornelia dodged the housekeeper's hand. "I'll hang it up later," she said, protective of the secret package hidden away in her pocket. "I'm still cold," she added lamely, and then she ran up the stairs.

When she got into her bedroom, she ripped the package open and found a book inside. Her heart gave a

happy little leap when she saw the book's title: *The Superior Person's Second Book of Weird and Wondrous
Words*. She rustled around in the package and un-
earthed a note from the bookstore on behalf of the
sender. With relish, Cornelia yanked the note out of its
little envelope. It read:

Dear Cornelia S.,

Another cache of words to add to your treasury.

With greatest affection,

V. S.

Cornelia was thrilled, for she had indeed exhausted
the first book. And this new one had come just at the
right time, since The Howling Dog was sure to require a
few vocabulary zingers that very evening. She was por-
ing over the pages when she heard Madame Desjardins
lumbering up the stairs. Cornelia crammed the package
under the bed and threw herself into her armchair with
an old book.

As usual, labored breathing from the climb accompanied the knock at the door. "A little sandwich for you,"
said Madame Desjardins as she came into the room and
set a tray on the desk.

"Thank you," said Cornelia, looking innocent.

"Tonight I am not going to be here," said Madame
Desjardins, clicking on the desk lamp, as per the daily

routine. "I will go to a concert with my niece in Brooklyn. It is planned a long time ago. Your mother will take you out to dinner, with Madame von Harding, probably."

Cornelia's heart sank. "Can't you order something for me, like Ingrid does?" she asked gloomily.

"*Non,*" said the housekeeper. "Madame Lucille says you are to go out."

Downstairs, Nina sang at full strength. Cornelia imagined her mother trapped in a room with a Category Five hurricane.

"Maybe you can pretend that you are sick, and she will stay at home for the evening," Madame Desjardins discreetly suggested, clearly feeling sorry for Cornelia.

"That never works," said Cornelia.

Madame Desjardins shrugged in agreement and patted Cornelia's head sympathetically. When she left the room and closed the door, Cornelia whipped out the new book from Virginia and studied it until the light from outside grew dim.

At around eight o'clock, the guttural wailing ceased downstairs and the doors of the music room opened.

"Cornelia!" Lucy called from the foot of the stairs. "Are you hungry, darling? We're going to Pastis—that restaurant in the Meatpacking District. You know, the one with the good French fries. Come downstairs now."

Cornelia pulled on her shoes slowly and trudged down the stairs with her coat under her arm. Lucy and

Nina talked in the kitchen. They didn't hear Cornelia come downstairs, so she delayed going in to greet them for as long as possible.

"Lucy, listen to me," Nina said. "It was bound to happen again sooner or later. He is a *very* attractive man, you know. And anyway, why should you care? He's been out of your life for years! Look how well you've done on your own! You've raised a child, even if she is an idiot savant, and you have an immortal career. You're practically Callas, honey, an absolute legend."

Cigarette smoke wafted into the hallway. "Well, it's still unpleasant to see him get married again," said Lucy in a wavering voice. "He doesn't even know what the words 'commitment' and 'responsibility' mean." She took a deep drag on her cigarette. "Well, at least the press has left me alone this time. Not like the last two times. I could barely even leave the building without some photographer from the *New York Post* leaping out at me like a mugger."

"Well, if you think *your* romantic life is bad, listen about mine, honey," Nina said, changing the subject. "I went out with that lawyer again last night. First he asked me if I've ever heard of Puccini, and then he told me that he was, quote, instrumental in bringing Polish ham to the Americas."

Cornelia had heard enough. She stalked into the kitchen to rescue her mother from Nina.

"Hello, you rebarbative hinny," said Cornelia to the singer, smiling sweetly. "Hinny" meant "the offspring of a female donkey and a male horse," and "rebarbative" meant "repulsive and off-putting." In response, Nina shot Cornelia a withering look.

Lucy suppressed a smile. She swept over to her daughter and kissed her on the forehead. "Let's go get something to eat, darling," she whispered into Cornelia's hair.

Twenty minutes later, Cornelia was stuffed into a booth with Lucy and Nina at Pastis. Cornelia propped the tall menu up on the table and stared at its contents. A waiter minced up to the table.

"I'll have the *escargots*," ordered Lucy. "And my daughter will have a hamburg—"

"No," interrupted Cornelia. "I would like the *moules, s'il vous plaît*, and a *chocolat chaud. Merci beaucoup.*" She had no idea what *moules* were, but if they were good enough for Virginia, they were good enough for her.

The waiter looked impressed as he whisked away the menus. Cornelia peeked shyly out of the corner of her eye to see if Lucy had noticed her sophisticated order.

Her mother stared at her. "Where did you learn those French food words?" she asked. "I don't remember seeing a French class on your report card."

Cornelia had her answer all ready. "From Madame Desjardins," she answered.

"Ah, of course," said Lucy, sipping a glass of water.

Nina looked as though she could care less whether Cornelia had ordered *moules* or a plate of fried rat. She slugged down a glass of champagne and turned to Lucy.

"Did you hear what Henri LeCroix did the other day?" she drawled. "It was the day before his big show at the Guggenheim. He ripped up every single one of his photographs that were supposed to hang in the exhibit! The museum was furious." She smeared some blood-red lipstick on her lips and patted them with a napkin. "I'm telling you, all artists are crazy."

"I heard a story about a crazy artist," Cornelia piped up, eager to divert her mother's attention.

Lucy looked as though she might die of shock. Cornelia never uttered an unnecessary word around Nina, unless it contained at least eight syllables and was designed to silence the singer instantly.

"Really? What story is that?" she asked.

Cornelia related the Picasso story that Virginia had told her several weeks before. She was careful to leave out all of the names, of course, but she was secretly pleased to see Lucy watching her, fascinated.

"I know that story," Nina butted in bossily. "It's a famous story about the Somerset sisters and Pablo Picasso. You know who those sisters are, Lucy, don't you?

One of them was a well-known writer, and two of them were painters. I think there was another one also. The fat one—what was her name? Gertrude or Gilda or something."

Cornelia's stomach shrank in horror when she heard this. How was she going to get out of this one now? She had never, in a million years, imagined that someone else would know about Virginia, much less about Alexandra, Beatrice, and Gladys. And anyway, the Picasso incident had taken place so long ago—how could Nina know about it? And then things got worse.

"Yes, they were from a very important family here in New York," Nina continued. "Their father was an extremely wealthy banker and philanthropist. I heard, incidentally, that one of those sisters—the writer—just moved into your building, Lucy. I think I read that in the *Times* or something. I meant to ask you if you'd seen her yet."

"Reallllly," said Lucy, looking intrigued. "We just had new tenants move in next door. I wonder if it's her. I'll ask Walter. Those women were so fascinating."

And then she peered down at Cornelia, who had slumped practically under the table with misery by that point. "Cornelia Street! Sit up straight," Lucy snapped. "Where did you hear about Picasso and the Somerset sisters?"

Tears threatened to spill down Cornelia's cheeks.

Lucy would soon learn that Virginia lived next door and would go over to see her, and that would be the end of the secret friendship. And to make things worse, Cornelia had brought this on herself. Why hadn't she just kept her mouth shut? It seemed that any time Cornelia said something that wasn't from her book of superior words, everything just went wrong. And with Lucy staring at her now, she blurted out the first thing that came to her mind.

"I saw something about them on TV," she whispered, her cheeks burning. "On the Entertainment Channel."

Lucy frowned. "I'm going to tell that Madame Desjardins not to watch those trashy shows in front of you," she said.

Just then, the waiter brought the food to the table. "Your *moules*, Mademoiselle," he said grandly as he set down a big dish of pungent mussels in front of Cornelia.

It was all too much. Cornelia hated seafood, and seeing the mussels and garlic steaming away under her nose was the last straw. Tears started to roll down her face.

After a few moments, Nina looked up from her endive salad. "Uh-oh—*somebody's* being a little dramatic," she said nastily. "*Now* what's wrong with you?"

"Cornelia!" Lucy said with great concern. "What's the matter?"

Cornelia didn't answer. She was afraid that if she

talked, the dam inside her would burst and she would really start crying.

After a few moments of cajoling and awkwardly soothing her daughter, Lucy realized that it was hopeless. "I'm going to take her home, Nina," she said, throwing some money down on the table. "She must be overtired or something. I'll call you tomorrow."

Nina could not have looked more horrified and wronged if Lucy had just run over her dog. "Don't call too early," she said sniffily as she allowed Lucy to peck her good-bye on the cheek.

Then the most unexpected thing happened.

Lucy and an upset Cornelia were hailing a taxi outside when suddenly a bright flash blinded them. Cornelia blinked several times before she could make out the figure of a photographer and a man with a pad of paper standing in front of her. Cornelia felt like Beatrice and Alexandra at Picasso's studio the night of the big party.

"Miz Englehart—I'm Dick Nugent from the *Daily News*," the man with the pad said, a cigarette dangling from his lower lip. "You got any comment on your ex-husband's newest wife? Look at the camera and say cheese." The camera flashed again as a taxi pulled up.

Lucy grabbed Cornelia and strode toward the taxi. "No comment," she told the reporter viciously. "Get out of here."

The man looked at Cornelia and beckoned to the photographer, who squatted in front of her and snapped her picture close up.

"Little girl," the reporter said. "Whaddya think about your playboy daddy getting married again? Maybe you'll get some new sisters and brothers."

Lucy pushed Cornelia into the taxi and slammed the door shut. Cornelia heard Lucy shouting at the top of her lungs at the man.

"Don't you ever, *ever* talk to my daughter again! Ever! Do you *understand* me?"

Cornelia watched in shock as her mother began to beat the reporter with her purse and fists. People on the street stopped and stared, and the photographer took pictures of the commotion until Lucy violently knocked his camera onto the sidewalk. Several waiters from the restaurant ran out and tried to pry her away from the men.

Lucy hit the reporter one more time for good measure and ran to the taxi. "Just *drive*," she yelled at the driver as she got in and banged the door shut behind her. "Go, go, go, go, *go*."

Breathing hard, her eyes wild and damp, Lucy looked over at Cornelia. "I'm so sorry about that, darling," she said as she lit a cigarette with trembling fingers. "Those men will never bother you again. Just forget all about what that reporter said to you."

And then she did something that she hadn't done since Cornelia was a little girl: she reached out and took Cornelia's hand.

The whole scene had completely bewildered Cornelia. She didn't understand what the reporter had been talking about, and she was still sickened at the prospect of having her friendship with Virginia discovered and changed forever. It had been a terrible night.

But just for the moment, in the leather cocoon of the yellow taxi, Cornelia just lay back and held her mother's hand, with its long, talented, famous fingers wrapped around her own.

The next day was Saturday, so Cornelia didn't have to wake up early for school. She slept for a long time, but she still felt bleary when she woke up. She padded downstairs in her pajamas. Madame Desjardins bustled her to the kitchen table and set down a croissant for her.

Lucy treaded down the stairs. She came into the kitchen wearing a silk bathrobe and poured herself a cup of coffee.

"Good morning, darling," Lucy said weakly. She was never particularly social in the morning. "How are you feeling this morning?"

"Fine," said Cornelia from behind a tall glass of orange juice. "But like I'm under water."

Lucy sipped her coffee. "I know how you feel," she

said, and walked over to the table. She kissed Cornelia absentmindedly on the forehead, and then walked out of the room. A minute later, she closed the door to the music room and plunked out a melancholy tune at the piano.

Cornelia chewed her croissant and thought about the night before. She couldn't believe that she'd almost let the cat out of the bag about Virginia. But maybe, she reasoned, things on this front weren't as bad as she'd thought in the restaurant. Even though Lucy knew that one of the Somerset sisters might be living in the building, what was the likelihood that she would really track Virginia down and visit her? After all, her mother was hardly ever here in the first place. Perhaps Cornelia had overreacted.

Furthermore, the incident with the reporter and photographer was getting strangely mixed up in her mind with Virginia's story about the reporters in Paris more than fifty years ago. Now in the daylight and with Lucy back in the music room, the whole incident didn't even seem real anymore. Cornelia finished her breakfast and ran upstairs to read.

It was an overcast March day. Later, after lunch, Cornelia went for a walk. She browsed around her usual haunts on Bleecker Street and stopped in at the Biography Bookshop. The owner greeted her enthusiastically.

"Look what we have here, Cornelia!" he said. "It just

arrived." He handed her a new book titled *The Greatest Pianists of Our Time.* "Both your mom and your dad are in it. Why don't you take this copy home with you? It's a present."

Cornelia thanked him and took the book across the street to a little park. She flipped through the pages until she came to the photographs in the middle. She recognized many of the performers' faces from her mother's cocktail parties: Alicia de Larrocha, André Watts, Murray Perahia. There was Gunner Joerg, the pianist who got drunk and fell on their Christmas tree one year. A photo of Lucy on page 178 showed her onstage at Carnegie Hall, the most famous concert hall in New York City.

And there, on page 182, was a photo of her father. The caption under the picture read: "Leonard Zajac Mazur performing at Alice Tully Hall on June 8, 2003."

She looked at his handsome face for similarities to her own but could see none. She knew that Leonard Zajac Mazur was her father, but he was a complete stranger. They didn't even have the same last name.

As she examined the picture, Cornelia thought about what the reporter had said to her at the restaurant. So her father was getting married again—that much was obvious. It shouldn't have made a difference to Cornelia one way or another, since he'd never been a part of her life in the first place—but the news bothered her. Why would he want a whole new wife and new children when he had a perfectly good daughter here in New York? Why didn't he want to live with her and Lucy in their big white apartment on Greenwich Street? Had Cornelia done something to drive him away? No, that wasn't possible, for she hadn't even been born yet when he left her mother.

Cornelia just didn't understand it. It seemed that everyone in the world wanted to get close to Lucy, except for Leonard Zajac Mazur. He clearly wanted to stay as far away from both of them as possible.

She closed the book and left it behind on the park bench for some lucky new owner.

When Cornelia got back to her building, she went straight to Virginia's front door and rang the doorbell. To Cornelia's disappointment, no one answered. She rang the bell again. Just as she was about to go back to her apartment, Patel whisked the door open.

"Oh, hello, Cornelia-ji," he said, holding the door open for her. "Please come in."

Cornelia came in and took off her shoes in the usual place next to the door. She glanced up at Patel and did a double take. He wore an apron colored with dashes of paint, and his fingernails were various shades of blue, brown, red, and yellow. Paintbrushes poked out of his apron pocket. Even his neat white turban had a smear of green paint on it.

"Virginia is in the library, I think," Patel reported. "Follow me."

"Patel, are you a famous painter like Picasso?" Cornelia asked, tagging along next to him as he led her to a door that she hadn't been through yet.

"No," he replied. "I am not that famous yet, but I am almost as good." He smiled at her benevolently.

"What are you painting?" Cornelia pressed.

Patel looked very mysterious. "You will find out soon, but not today," he answered after a pause. "It will be a nice surprise." He knocked on the door in front of them. "Virginia-ji is writing today," he informed Cornelia.

"Come in," called Virginia distractedly from the other side of the door. "Oh! It's you, Cornelia. Thank you, Patel."

Cornelia trotted into the room and was once again transported to another era and place. This time, she felt like she had entered an ancient library filled with secrets and knowledge. Tall, dark wood bookshelves towered to the ceiling all around her. Every sort of book imaginable crammed the shelves: novels, novellas, epics, biographies, autobiographies, encyclopedias, and atlases. There were books of plays, poems, fables, myths, limericks, and short stories; tomes about history, war, art, and music. On the slices of wall between the bookshelves hung gigantic paintings of racehorses and castles. Magnificent chairs with gargoyles protruding from their wood frames were arranged in clusters around the room. A chess set made of crystal shone on top of a round leather table, its pieces standing in four straight lines and waiting silently for battle.

And of course, a black-and-white picture of the young Somerset sisters sat on one of the shelves. This time, the ladies stood in front of an airplane with propellers, and they wore leather flying helmets and goggles.

Virginia sat behind an ancient-looking black typewriter on top of an immense mahogany desk. She wore a dark blue scarf turban-style around her head, and a huge sparkling sapphire necklace glistened at the base of her throat. She had a pencil tucked behind her ear, and her elegant fingers stretched across the keyboard of the typewriter. A neat stack of paper sat on either side of the machine. Mister Kinyatta, who seemed to be getting lazier every time Cornelia came to visit, slumbered under the desk. He lay snoring on his back with all four paws folded in the air and his jowls hanging back to reveal his teeth. A small green desk lamp provided the only light in the room.

"It's a little dark in here, I know," Virginia said to Cornelia. "Sorry about that. I always write in a dark room. If I'm near a window, I get so easily distracted, as you know. Anyway, welcome to my English library! I modeled it after a room in the famous Bodleian Library at Oxford University, which is many hundreds of years old."

Cornelia walked along the edges of the room, running her fingers over the bindings of the books. "I love it in here," she said, feeling immediately at home.

"You'll love it even more in a moment," said Virginia. "Look over there." And she pointed across the room from her.

Then Cornelia saw the floor-to-ceiling bookshelf of dictionaries Virginia had told her about on the first day of their acquaintance. She had never seen so many books about words, not even at the bookstore on Bleecker Street. Row after row of dictionaries in English, French, German, Spanish, Hebrew, Portuguese, Italian, Russian, and even Greek and Arabic. There were dozens of them, some of them old with crumbling gilded edges and bindings, and others with new taut canvas covers. Cornelia stood on her tiptoes to peruse all of them.

"They're beautiful," Cornelia exclaimed, more excited than Virginia had ever seen her. "Oh! And thank you very much for the new book. It already came in handy."

"You're very welcome," said Virginia. "I know it's a lot

to learn, but a girl has to work hard to stay at the top of her game."

Cornelia sat down in a particularly big wooden chair, which reminded her of the Moroccan bride's throne. "Are you working on your new idea?" she asked Virginia. "And what's it about again?" she added, hoping that Virginia would slip up and tell her about the novel.

"Ingenious ploy, Cornelia S.," said Virginia. "In other words, nice try. You *know* that it's a secret. But I'll tell you this much: it's a wonderful story. It's very sad at moments, but filled with hope and promise underneath."

"Wow," said Cornelia. "Did you get your idea from spying with your binoculars?"

"Not this time," responded Virginia. "I was inspired by something else. Why don't you stay here and read while I finish this chapter. Once I'm on a roll, I have to keep going or I'll forget what I was going to say." And she began to clack away on the raised, shaky keys of the old typewriter.

Cornelia trolled the shelves for a book to read and selected an aged copy of *King Arthur and His Knights of the Round Table.* She learned that the story of King Arthur was one of the most famous myths of England, and no one knows even now if he and his sidekicks ever really existed. The pages were made of fine fabric, and gold-laced painted illustrations of Sir Lancelot, Merlin, and Guinevere accompanied the text. Cornelia curled up in a large leather armchair, drowsy and secure in the warm library.

She read and Virginia wrote until the light began to fade around the edges of the drawn curtain over the window. Cornelia leaped up when she realized how much time had passed. Virginia stopped her feverish typing and looked up.

"Oh, are you leaving, Cornelia?" she asked, still clearly in another world. "Would you like to come back and read with me again tomorrow?"

Cornelia nodded. She went back every day that week.

That Sunday, Madame Desjardins pulled out Lucy's suitcases again. This time, Lucy was going off to England to give a recital at Buckingham Palace with The Howling Dog. They had been practicing for days. Sometimes while Cornelia stowed away in Virginia's library, Nina hit a particularly high note in the apartment next door and Mister Kinyatta would leap up and growl. When Lucy and Nina finally left for London, everyone in the building seemed grateful.

Cornelia tiptoed into Virginia's library that afternoon and picked up her King Arthur book. Virginia looked up at her from her usual spot at the desk.

"It's awfully quiet this afternoon over there in the Englehart apartment," Virginia said. "I bet that The

Howling Dog has been arrested for creating a public disturbance and was hauled off to jail—am I right?" Cornelia had told Virginia about Nina's secret nickname several days earlier.

"No," said Cornelia, sitting down and opening her book. "They left for England this morning, to give a concert for the royal family."

"Well, I'm sure the queen will never forget the experience," Virginia said naughtily. She squinted at Cornelia's book. "What's that you're reading?"

"King Arthur," Cornelia said. "It's about this famous king who lived hundreds of years ago in England, and he had lots of adventures with some knights who sat at a round table."

Virginia smiled. "I am very familiar with the legend of King Arthur," she said. "In fact, the Somerset sisters may be among the few people in this age who have something of a personal connection to him."

"What do you mean?" asked Cornelia, sitting up straight. Virginia was awfully unpredictable for an adult.

"It's a long story," Virginia sighed, looking down at her typewriter. "I don't want to bore you with it." She peeked up to see if Cornelia had taken the bait, which of course she had.

"I won't be bored," protested Cornelia. "Please tell me! Madame Desjardins is making *cassoulet* for dinner, which takes hours. I have all afternoon."

"Well, in *that* case, I have several stories for you," said Virginia, looking very vibrant all of the sudden. "They take place in England, where we lived after we left Paris. As you would expect, we got into an equal amount of trouble there."

"You and your sisters were such reprobates," giggled Cornelia. "Reprobate" meant "wrongdoer."

"Oh, we weren't *criminals* or anything," Virginia said. "We were just *lively*." She leaned back in her chair and crossed her hands on her stomach. "Hmmm. Speaking of the queen, did you know that she personally banned Gladys from the country at one point? Listen to this."

And she began to tell her story.

Chapter Eight

England, 1953

"Alexandra, Beatrice, Gladys, and I left our lovely, hidden, vine-covered house in Paris after the Picasso incident and took a ship across the English Channel to England. Gladys almost refused to come along because it was against British law to bring foreign dogs into the country. We'd have to put our four Messieurs in an English quarantine facility for six months before they could come to live with us in London. But in the end, we persuaded Gladys by promising to visit the dogs at least once a week.

"In England, they speak the same language as us—English, naturally—but we still had to translate many things. They have different words for things there than we do here in New York."

"I know," said Cornelia. "Walter says 'lift' instead of 'elevator.'"

"And here we say 'bathroom,' but there they say 'water closet' or 'loo,'" said Virginia. "And 'lorry' instead of 'truck.' It confused us, and for the first time, we had no phrase book to help us. Everything was just slightly different. Being an American in England is like being a piece in a puzzle that almost fits—but not quite."

"When we arrived in London, we took our luggage to a place called the Oxford and Cambridge University Club, a famous old private club and hotel. Our father, who had gone to Oxford University when he was our age, had arranged for us to stay there. It had a huge marble staircase and a seemingly endless list of bars with names like the Marlborough Room, the King Edward VII Room, the Pall Mall Room, and the Smoking Room. The club's members were surrounded by bookshelves jammed with old books; paintings of dukes, earls, queens, and kings now long dead; old clocks ticking and dinging quietly away; and, of course, lots of pictures of the ancient buildings of Oxford and Cambridge Universities.

"The manager of the hotel, Mr. Snell, came out to greet us when we arrived. Lumpy as an old mattress, he had a shining dome of a bald head and a great beaklike nose. He wore a loose three-piece suit and said things like 'Oh, rather' and 'Jolly good' all the time.

"'Ah, the little Somerset girls,' he said. His voice seemed to come from somewhere deep inside his beak. 'Welcome. Your father is one of our most illustrious members. My, how you all resemble him! Well, maybe not *you*,' he added as he looked Gladys up and down. 'In his honor, I have arranged for you to stay in his two favorite suites, which overlook Big Ben and the Houses of Parliament.'

"Then he looked discreetly around, and said in a lower voice, 'Now, just so you know, this club is for gentlemen only. Usually ladies have to stay in the little house next door. But for the Somerset girls we have made an exception. We would appreciate your discretion in this matter, you do understand? Jolly good.'

"And with that, Mr. Snell tapped a little bell on the counter and about ten bellboys scurried over to collect our bags.

"We followed our caravan of luggage up the grand staircase to our rooms. Naturally, the twins shared one room and Gladys and I shared the other. Gladys threw herself onto one of the beds.

"'What was that elephant Mr. Snell talking about downstairs?' she said crabbily. Alexandra and Beatrice came into our room and closed the door.

"'He meant that we're not allowed to tell the club members that we're staying here, or let any of them see us,' said Alexandra. 'I just read in my guidebook that women aren't usually allowed in at all.'"

"Why couldn't women join the club?" interjected Cornelia.

"That's just the way things were back then," said Virginia. "For hundreds of years, men thought that women and children should be seen and not heard. And as you now know, such meekness was *hardly* an attribute of the Somerset sisters. And Mr. Snell expected us to make ourselves invisible while we stayed at the club!"

"That's the dumbest thing I've ever heard," said Cornelia.

"That's what we thought too," Virginia replied. "As you'll soon see."

"'How uncivilized,' commented Gladys disapprovingly. 'Well, I don't know about the rest of you, but I'm too hungry to think about this now. Let's go downstairs and get something to eat.'

"We trampled down the stairs. 'There's the dining room, I think,' said Beatrice, veering into a big wood-paneled room. Many men sat at round tables, smoking pipes, playing cards and chess, and reading newspapers. Sunlight filtered in through the shuttered windows and made bright, hazy lines in the smoky air. When we walked in, all of the club members stopped what they were doing and stared at us.

"'I say,' said one man with a big mustache. 'Can we help you? Are you lost, ladies?'

"'I say, old boy,' said Gladys, somewhat rudely. 'We're looking for the dining room.'

"An uncomfortable silence followed, and the gray Mr. Snell appeared as if by magic at the door. Uttering an 'Oh, rather,' he hastily ushered us out.

"As soon as we were out of the room, his gracious smile faded and he said, 'Girls—off to the ladies' luncheon room with you.' And he bustled us like naughty puppies out to the street and into an ugly house next door. Five minutes later, we found ourselves in a bright fuchsia-pink dining room in the new house.

"'I'm sure you'll find everything you need here,' said Mr. Snell, and he strode back out to the gentlemen's section of the club.

"'This room is the color of Pepto-Bismol,' said Gladys, looking around with disdain. 'It's making me lose my appetite. I've had enough of this place already, and we only just got here.'

"'What's so great about that stupid club anyway?' Beatrice asked crossly. 'After all, those men were hardly having a top-secret meeting about the atom bomb. They were just sitting around, doing all the boring things men do in their living rooms every day of the week.'

"The waiter plopped down four dishes in front of us. I examined our fare, which consisted of several shrimp drowning in a vat of mayonnaise."

"How putrescent," Cornelia commented under her breath.

"The club's specialty," Virginia said, and went on.

"'Excuse me,' called Gladys to the waiter. 'Can you take this back to the kitchen? I'll have a big juicy steak instead. Thanks, old chap.'

"'I'm afraid that steak is served only in the gentlemen's part of the club,' sniffed the waiter, snatching her plate away and leaving Gladys's place empty. We looked at each other in disbelief and reached for the bread basket.

"'I have an idea,' Gladys told me later that afternoon, back in our suite. 'I'm going out for a bit. I'll be back shortly.' And she pulled on her shoes and coat and left the room.

"About two hours later, she came back loaded down with shopping bags and called for a Somerset conference.

"'Ladies,' she declared, putting her hands on her hips. 'We are going to do a little detective work this evening. Remember when we wore the *haiks* in the *souk* in Morocco? Tonight we're going on another undercover mission in a different disguise.' And out of one of the bags she pulled a man's suit and a tall evening hat. 'That one's for you, Virginia.'

"'Gladys—have you gone nuts?' asked Alexandra.

"'I just want to see what the big deal is,' Gladys said. 'What can possibly be so fascinating about the club that women aren't allowed in? So, we're going to camouflage ourselves and investigate.'

"She shoved one of her stout legs into the pants of a suit. 'These are from that Harrods store, by the way, so they are of very good quality,' she added. 'Nothing but the best for the Somerset gentlemen.'

"'Gladys,' I said practically. 'I'm sure that these suits are top-notch. But don't you think that they'll recognize our *faces* below the brims and above the collars?'

"'Ho, ho!' Gladys said, zipping up her suit pants and looping a tie through her shirt collar. 'You guys must think that I'm really dumb. Of *course* I've already thought of that, and have addressed our needs accordingly. Look in that bag over there.'

"Fifteen minutes later, I walked with my sisters down the grand staircase wearing a suit, a tall hat, and a fake mustache plastered to my upper lip, which I was sure would slip off at any moment.

"Gladys, being the glutton that she was, had gone one step further and slathered a fake beard onto her chin below her mouth. She gummed a pipe as a horse chomps its bit.

"'My mustache is loose,' Beatrice whispered. 'I can't believe that you talked us into this.'

"When we reached the bottom, Gladys looked around to make sure that no one was looking at us. 'I brought this down with us as well,' she said, fishing a little tube of something out of her pocket. 'For our mustaches, in case they start to fall off.'

"We peered down at the item. Its label proclaimed:

ENGLAND'S MOST POPULAR INDUSTRIAL-STRENGTH GLUE! POWERFUL AS THE ROYAL NAVY, MIGHTY AS THE BRITISH ARMY!

"'Don't be absurd, Gladys!' hissed Alexandra impatiently. 'Shoemakers and handymen use this stuff—it's probably toxic! Put it away this instant.' Gladys shrugged and put the glue into the back pocket of her pants.

"We marched into the Smoking Room. The usual suspects were there, smoking, talking, playing cards, and reading. Several of them nodded at us as we sat down around one of the tables. One of them burst into laughter at another's joke, and his sharp 'Rah, rah, rah!' set my nerves on edge. A waiter planted himself in front of our table and peered down at us snootily.

"'May I help you?' he sniveled.

"'Four whishkeys and shodas,' Gladys said gruffly, her teeth gritted around her pipe. The waiter nodded, examining us suspiciously, and walked to the bar.

"'All right—start eavesdropping, gentlemen,' Alexandra whispered to us once the drinks had been set down on our table. She tried to press her mustache onto her lip as inconspicuously as possible.

"I strained my ears to make out a conversation at the next table. It went something like this:

Gentleman Number One (with walrus mustache, round glasses, and a big, fat red face): I say, I hear that the cricket match on Sunday will be something to behold!

Gentleman Number Two (with a wan, thin little face and a big Adam's apple bobbing up and down in his throat): Oh, rather. You don't say.

Gentleman Number One (reaching for his pipe): It was most riveting last year. Such fine sportsmanship, such fine show-manship. It is such a shame the game only lasts for three days. It should go on for at least a week.

Gentleman Number Two (nodding in agreement): Oh, rather. I quite agree.

"I'm telling you, Cornelia, there are mummies buried in Egypt who were less bored than I was by that conversation. But now we were stuck sitting there at our table, eavesdropping away on our stodgy fact-finding mission.

"'I have to take this thing off,' whispered Beatrice, who had been listening to a different group of men. 'It refuses to stay on my lip. And if I have to hear one more thing about last Saturday's fox hunt in Sussex, I'm going to paste my mustache across that man's mouth.'

"'Okay, boys, let's go,' said Gladys. 'I think that we've learned everything we need to know.'

"We got up from our chairs. Alexandra, Beatrice, and I were almost out the door when we realized that Gladys wasn't with us. She was still sitting in her chair. Exasperated, Alexandra walked back to the table.

"'*Mr.* Gladys, will you be joining us?' she asked. Gladys whispered something up to Alexandra, whose eyes bulged. She walked back to us quickly.

"'Gladys is stuck in the chair,' she reported to Beatrice and me. 'That glue must have come undone in her back pocket. Getting her up and out—without getting kicked out of the club ourselves, not to mention getting our *father* kicked out—is going to be a considerable challenge.'

"We walked back to the table, where Gladys bucked around in her chair. After a brief, discreet conference at the table, we concluded that there was nothing left to do but create a diversion and rip Gladys out of the chair when everyone looked in the other direction.

"'I'm not doing it this time,' said Alexandra. 'I distracted everyone in Marrakech, during the Moroccan wedding affair.'

"'Well,' said Beatrice. 'My mustache is practically falling off. If I'm the official Distractor, it will *definitely* fall off and we'll be found out. That leaves *you*, Virginia.'

"My heart sank, but Gladys looked so miserable under her beard that I promised to think of something. Just then, the snobby waiter caught my eye and I got an idea.

"'Get ready,' I whispered to my sisters as I walked across the room. I stood near the fireplace mantel next to the front entrance of the room and pretended to admire the pictures hanging there. 'Jolly good, aren't they?' I said in a deep voice to a gentleman who had been examining me from a nearby table. He looked back at his newspaper. The snobby waiter stood at the bar, piling a tray high with whiskey-filled tumblers. As luck would have it, he came in my direction.

"'Gah!!!!!!!!!!!!!!' he screamed as he spilled over my outstretched foot.

"The glasses flew off his tray and the whiskey splashed all over a stern-looking bulldog of a man who had just walked into the room. From across the room came the sharp sound of fabric ripping accompanied by an unladylike squawk. Every gentleman shot out of his seat in alarm.

"Mr. Snell rushed in. 'Oh, my heavens—what is happening?' he said, not knowing where to look first. The snooty waiter lay sprawled facedown on the floor. Whiskey dripped down the walls, chairs, and the front of the bulldog man standing in the doorway.

"'Oh, my goodness!' shouted Mr. Snell, snatching a napkin away from another waiter and frantically wiping down the guest's suit. 'Mr. Churchill, sir, I am terribly, terribly sorry! What a dreadful mistake! I cannot apologize enough, sir.'

"The man batted Mr. Snell away with a large paw. 'What a waste of good whiskey,' he said. 'Fool,' he said to the waiter on the floor as he stepped over him. 'I'll have some in a glass this time,' he added to everyone in general. He stumped over to a big leather chair near the fireplace and lit a cigar.

"Mr. Snell turned his attention to the overturned table across the room and found a whole new reason to look horrified. Beatrice and Alexandra were heaving Gladys up from the floor. When they had ripped her off the chair, Gladys's legs had kicked out and upset the table, which lay on its side. The seat of her pants still stuck to the chair and her beard dangled from her chin.

"Mr. Snell turned a furious bright red, from the shiny curve at the top of his bald head to the end of his beak and down his neck. '*Gentlemen,*' he said sarcastically, trembling all over. 'I take it that you will be checking out of the Oxford and Cambridge University Club this evening. Shall we send your bill to a Mr. Augustus P. Somerset in New York City, or will you be paying it yourselves?'

"And that was the end of our stay at the club, and unfortunately, it was the end of our father's membership there as well. But we figured that he was better off without it. We certainly were. We wore our suits, hats, and mustaches as we happily checked out an hour later."

"I still have that mustache, you know," said Virginia. "I kept it as a souvenir, although it's in tatters now. I wore it to feminist rallies in the 1970s, but I don't think anyone quite appreciated it."

"Didn't your dad get mad at you?" Cornelia asked.

"Yes, to put it mildly," Virginia answered. "An absolute avalanche of angry telegrams flooded across the Atlantic for a week. After that, our parents arranged for us to go to the English countryside, so we would stay out of trouble."

"Did it work?"

Virginia smiled. "Now, what do you think?" she said. "Here's story number two."

"'I'm going to learn how to fly a plane,' Beatrice declared from behind the book she was reading.

"'Beatrice,' Alexandra said incredulously. 'You can't even ride a *bicycle*. And remember when you drove your scooter into that orange stand when you were six? And your accident with the roller skates?'

"Unfazed, Beatrice put the book down. Its cover had a picture of a young woman wearing an old-fashioned flying helmet and goggles.

"'That was *years* ago,' she said. 'I'd be much better at it now. I want to be like the pilot I'm reading about: Amelia Earhart. Except that day she went out flying and disappeared into the ocean. I could probably do without that part.'

"At the time this conversation took place, we had moved into a little seaside cottage in Cornwall, the beautiful and dramatic countryside in the southwest part of England. At night when we went to bed, the waves crashing on the craggy coast lulled us to sleep. In the morning, we woke to the cries of seagulls. It was autumn by then, so we had the lonely beaches to ourselves most of the time.

"Beatrice walked to the closest village the next day and inquired about flying lessons. When she came home, she proudly announced, 'It's all arranged. I start my classes tomorrow. There's a man with a small passenger plane who lives in the country who will teach me.'

"We tried to talk Beatrice out of it, but to no avail. She left for the airfield the next morning before the rest of us were even up for breakfast. Several weeks went by, and every morning she dutifully went off to her lessons. To our surprise and relief, nothing disastrous happened. Then one afternoon, she walked into our house carrying a box. She dropped it with a clatter on the kitchen table.

"'I've mastered the art of taking off and landing,' she announced. 'And now it's time to have some fun. I'm taking you on an airplane tour of the Cornwall coast tomorrow, ladies.' She opened the box and took out a soft leather flying helmet, which she tossed to me.

"'I'm not going up in that plane with you,' I said. 'So just forget about it.'

"Beatrice tossed helmets to Gladys and Alexandra as well. Alexandra examined hers. 'Is it an open-top plane?' she asked.

"'No,' Beatrice answered as she rummaged around in the box, eventually extracting several sets of goggles.

"'Then why do we need helmets and goggles?' Gladys asked, clearly getting into the spirit of the adventure. She pulled a pair of goggles over her eyes and adjusted the strap.

"'For the photos, of course,' Beatrice said matter-of-factly. The last item in the box was a beleaguered-looking old camera she'd bought at an antique store. 'We have to be at the field tomorrow at three o'clock sharp.'

"Of course, I found myself crammed into a car with my sisters the next afternoon, heading toward the airfield. Beatrice's flying teacher, a little man named Mr. Hardcastle, waited for us there. Gladys popped out of the car and marched right up to him.

"'Tell us the truth—can Beatrice fly this thing or not?' she demanded, pointing at the plane in the middle of the field. She peered down at him. 'I'll know if you're lying,' she added menacingly.

"Mr. Hardcastle put up his hands as if protecting himself from Gladys. 'Yes, yes, I assure you that she can fly it,' he stammered.

"We put on our goggles and helmets and posed in front of the plane. Mr. Hardcastle fumbled with the ancient camera. After what seemed like a century, the camera emitted a rusty, reluctant click. Then we hopped into the plane. Mr. Hardcastle waited until we were all buckled in, then closed the flimsy door.

"'Aren't you getting in too?' I shrieked to Mr. Hardcastle as Beatrice started the noisy motor. The propellers on the wings began to spin.

"Mr. Hardcastle cupped his hands around his mouth. 'There isn't room,' he shouted over the racket. 'Don't worry—you'll be fine,' he yelled as the plane jerked forward.

"'Ha!' said Gladys, who sat in the front of the plane next to Beatrice. 'Famous last words.'

"I tightened my seat belt until I could barely

breathe, and my stomach clenched into a ball as the plane bumped across the field. Just when I was sure that Beatrice would crash us into a patch of trees at the field's end, the plane's nose tilted upward and we took off into the sky. The ground fell away from us quickly.

"We flew through white cloud wisps that tangled and then disintegrated around the little plane. The farmhouses and villages below looked like toy buildings from the sky, and lush green fields stretched all the way to the horizon. Eventually the stern, dark blue sea came into view and we flew up along the coast. Enormous jagged cliffs—which in the summertime had been covered in purple sea lavender and pink thrift—lined the beaches. Even I had to admit that Beatrice was doing a good job, and I relaxed and enjoyed the ride.

"Just then, the plane began to sputter. 'Something is wrong!' Beatrice shouted. 'We had a full tank of fuel when we got into the plane, and now it's only half full! No—wait—less than that!'

"Gladys craned her neck to examine the panels in front of Beatrice. 'There must be some sort of hole in the fuel tank,' she hollered. 'And it looks like it's draining pretty quickly!'

"'Beatrice!' I cried. 'You have to land the plane this instant! Before the tank runs out entirely!' Alexandra looked as though she might throw up.

"Beatrice looked frantically out the window, assessing the terrain. Low trees and thick brambles covered the clifftops, making it impossible to land there.

"'We're going to have to land on the beach!' she yelled, her face as white as chalk. 'I think I see a stretch that's long enough to land on!'

"The plane jerked around wildly as Beatrice tilted it downward toward the shore. Gladys yelled things like, 'To the left! Now to the right! Thatta girl! Almost there!' And then, 'Ouff!' as the wheels of the plane hit the sand.

"I almost flew into Alexandra's lap despite the death grip my seat belt had on me. The plane swerved from side to side and sand flew up against the windows. We finally ground to a halt and the plane shuddered and died."

Cornelia sat on the edge of her seat. "What happened? Were you hurt? What about the plane?"

"To be honest, when we went down, I thought that it was the end of the Somerset sisters," Virginia said. "But except for a few bruises and cuts, all four of us were okay. It was a miracle. The plane, on the other hand, was toast. We had to run across the beach right away, in case any of the remaining fuel caught on fire and blew up the wreckage."

Cornelia's heart pounded in her chest. "It's like a movie," she said.

"It's *better* than a movie, my friend," said Virginia.

"We huddled next to the cliff walling in the deserted beach and took stock of our situation. Cold air blew in off the ocean, and the sun sank toward the horizon.

"'We don't even know where we are,' wailed Beatrice, her arms wrapped around herself.

"'We can't be that far away from civilization,' I said. 'Let's look for a way up this bluff before it gets too dark to see properly.' We stalked around the bottom of the cliff, looking for the easiest path to the top.

"'I think I found some old stairs!' shouted Alexandra, pointing to a very muddy, barely visible old stone staircase carved into the rocky precipice. Some of the stairs were badly eroded and dense moss covered the others.

"'We'll have to be extra careful,' said Gladys. 'Once we go up, it's a long way to fall down.'

"So we clawed our way up the slippery cliff on all fours like animals. By then, the sun had set and I shivered uncontrollably as I surveyed the land at the top of the cliff. A rugged plain of brambles and thorny trees stretched out for miles in front of us.

"'Let's start walking,' said Alexandra. 'I'm sure that I saw a few houses in the distance when we were coming in to land. Also, we'll stay warmer if we keep moving.'

"We stumbled across the tops of the cliffs as night fell. Gladys lurched along about twenty feet behind us, and finally sat down on an old broken stone wall.

"'I don't see anything up ahead,' she complained. 'And one of us is going to twist her ankle by stepping in some grass-covered hole in the ground. Mr. Hardcastle and the police will come looking for us soon. I vote that we stay put, light a fire here so they can find us, and keep warm.'

"Coming from Gladys, it sounded like a shockingly logical idea. My fingertips and toes were numb by then, and the darkness seemed to be swallowing us up. A slender sliver of a moon rose from the ocean.

"We gathered a little pile of damp, sandy sticks and lit a fire with some matches Gladys had in her back pocket. The flames gradually grew taller as we huddled together to stay warm.

"'Look around us,' whispered Beatrice, as though someone might overhear us on that desolate plain. 'It looks like we're sitting in some sort of ruin. Do you see all of those crumbled stone walls?'

"Gladys lumbered around the site with a lit match. 'It looks like this was a big room once,' she said. 'I can see the remains of all four walls. And I can just make out more walls going down the hill, and that looks like a turret over there. There's another one!'

"We all got up and explored in the weak moonlight, and discovered many more walls, most of them covered in moss and dead, winter-bare brambles of lavender. Suddenly I remembered reading about the ruins of a very famous old castle on the coast of Cornwall.

"'I know where we are!' I exclaimed, my voice getting lost in the wind coming over the bluffs. 'This is Tintagel! You know—one of King Arthur's castles!'

"My sisters looked at me blankly. 'Do you mean *the* King Arthur, of Knights of the Round Table fame?' Gladys asked incredulously.

"I nodded. 'He was supposedly born at this very spot, more than a thousand years ago,' I said. The wind howled around us more strongly than before and a chill settled into my bones.

"We all came back and clustered together around the fire again. Soon Alexandra got up to collect more twigs. She walked into the darkness, down toward the ridge, and came scurrying back to us a few minutes later.

"'Come look at this!' she whispered hoarsely. 'You'll never believe it! It looks like there is some sort of *play* happening on the next bluff!'

"'What do you mean, a play? It's freezing out here, and it must be midnight!' Gladys exclaimed.

"We followed her over the crumbling parapets to the ridge. To my complete surprise, Alexandra was right. A group of men moved about the bluff below, and like us, they had lit a small bonfire. I strained my eyes in the dark and counted at least twenty of them, all dressed in what looked like costumes of faded suits of armor. They threw wood onto the fire and kneeled on the ground, examining a big piece of paper. They argued and made gestures in the air as they talked.

"'What on earth are they doing?' asked Beatrice. 'And why are they dressed like that? I know it's cold up here, but *really*.'

"'I'm telling you—it has to be a strange theater company, practicing an outdoor play or something,' Alexandra said. 'Anyway, they look more local than we do. They can probably help us get out of here—but this ridge is too steep for us to climb down. They'll have to come up somehow and get us. Hello!' she called out to the men. 'Up here! Hello!' She waved her arms in the air. The wind picked up, drowning her out.

"'Try lighting a bunch of matches at once!' I said. 'Maybe the flare will get their attention.'

"Beatrice tried to light the matches, but they behaved like damp sticks and refused to spark. 'That's weird,' she said. 'They were lighting up just fine a few minutes ago. Let's try yelling all at once and maybe they'll hear us over the wind.'

"We all started leaping up and down and shouting. The actors ignored us. Finally, we created such a racket that one of them looked up at us. He turned away from their fire and seemed to float in our direction. As he got closer, we could see the details of his costume. A small man with a beard and long hair, he wore a magnificent breastplate of armor and a tall crown. He stopped at the bottom of the ridge and stared up at us. His hypnotic gaze quelled even Gladys into silence.

"He slowly lifted a long, elegant finger to his lips

and whispered, 'Shush'—a long, low sound. It was as windy as ever, but his whisper was as clear as church bells on a Sunday morning. He turned his back to us and walked back to the fire.

"'Well!' said Alexandra. 'How rude! I know that rehearsal time for plays is important—but we're freezing up here! If they won't help us, who will?'

"We watched the men in astonishment for a while. They seemed to be plotting something, and kept consulting the paper. We must have sat there like that for hours, surveying their activities, for the next thing I knew, the sky began to fill with a pale blue morning light. I realized that I'd nodded off. Gladys, Beatrice, and Alexandra slept in a bundle next to me.

"The men on the bluff had disappeared, along with their paper. Not a trace of them remained. They had even meticulously cleared away the charred firewood from their bonfire.

"When my sisters woke up, we groggily walked across the bluffs again, searching for a town or a house. Finally, around noon, we spotted a huge old hotel sitting on a high cliff, overlooking the ocean. Overjoyed, we ran up the front stairs and into the lobby. The door creaked open on its ancient hinges.

"The place was empty. We rang the bell at the front desk, and the tinny little *ting* echoed through the lobby and down the hallway. Finally, a door swung open at the end of the corridor and the littlest old man I've ever seen walked through it. His shoes squeaked as he walked toward us.

"'Can we use your phone, please?' Beatrice cried, eager to call Mr. Hardcastle and the police to tell them we were still alive. The man pointed toward a cobweb-covered phone booth in the hallway. Beatrice ran over to it and began dialing. In the meantime, Alexandra and Gladys told the tiny man about our plane crash and escape across the bluffs.

"'And on top of everything else,' Gladys said, 'we saw some theater company out on the cliffs, wearing armor and practicing for a play—and none of the men would come up and help us! And I thought this was the spot where knightly chivalry originated!'

"The man got an odd look on his face. 'That's funny,' he said, his voice croaking with the effort of being used. 'There's no theater around here for many miles. No theater company either.'

"'But we saw actors dressed up in old costumes,' I said. 'And one was wearing a crown. He even told us to be quiet while they rehearsed.'

"The old man looked at us intently. 'No,' he said finally. 'There haven't been any actors around here for a long time. I suppose you saw old Arthur and his lads at it again. They like to show up out on the bluffs with their map from time to time, you know. Try not to bother them next time, lassies. They've got important work to do.'

"And with that, he squeaked back down the hallway and through the door at the end of it. Except for the sound of Beatrice shouting into the phone, the hotel was still and silent again."

Cornelia gripped the sides of her chair. "Do you mean that they really *were* ghosts this time?"

"What other conclusion can be drawn?" asked Virginia. "Over the next few weeks, we asked everyone in Cornwall about what we'd seen. Most of them shook their heads and said things to us like, 'Yer all crazy Yanks.' And then, when we went back with Mr. Hardcastle to survey the wreckage of the plane, we climbed up to the site of their campfire. I didn't see a single ash or footprint.

"So, finally we had to agree with the old man at the hotel that we'd seen the ghosts of King Arthur and his knights planning one of their famous battles in the ruins of Tintagel. Nobody else ever believed our story."

"I believe it," said Cornelia. She got up and tickled Mister Kinyatta. "I bet *you* believe it too, don't you, Mister Kinyatta?" He grunted and licked her hand.

"Well, dogs are supposed to be able to see ghosts a lot better than people can," said Virginia. "The Messieurs probably would have gone crazy if they'd been out on the Cornwall bluffs with us that night."

"I bet you missed them while they were in quarantine," said Cornelia.

"It was *terrible* being without those little beasts," answered Virginia. "Despite our visits, Gladys literally counted the days until we could go and get them from the kennel. And then, when they came home, they caused the biggest debacle of our visit to England."

"Why? What did they do?" Cornelia could hardly imagine Mister Kinyatta or his kin causing an international disaster.

"It was Gladys's fault, of course," said Virginia. "As usual."

"We moved back to London just after we fetched Messieurs Un, Deux, Trois, and Quatre from quarantine. Then the four Somersets and the four Messieurs moved into a big white house on Sloane Square.

"One afternoon at teatime, as we ate scones and jam, Alexandra scooped up Monsieur Deux and placed him on her lap.

"'Who's the most handsome dog in all of England?' she cooed at him, feeding him some crumbs from her plate. 'You are!' She lightly poked his stubby nose with her finger. Monsieur Deux stuck out his pink little tongue and panted. The other dogs didn't pay any attention as they busily scavenged for tidbits under the table.

"'Now that I think about it,' Alexandra declared, 'Monsieur Deux probably *is* the best-looking dog in England. I think we should enter him in that famous English dog show. What's it called again? The Crufts Dog Show.'

"'Ha!' said Gladys, her mouth full of scone. 'He'd

never win! Look at him! His eyes are practically going in opposite directions!'

"'He looks like a little alien,' laughed Beatrice, reaching over to pet him.

"'Or a stumpy caboose at the end of a train,' I volunteered.

"All of the good-natured ridicule only steeled Alexandra's resolve. A few days later, she walked into the tearoom with a big white envelope. 'Monsieur Deux has been invited to participate in the Crufts Dog Show,' she announced. 'And what's more, the queen of England herself will be there. One of her dogs, a Welsh corgi, is going to compete as well.'

"We all looked with surprise at Monsieur Deux, who napped away unsuspectingly on a nearby couch. He rasped and drooled in his sleep.

"Alexandra went into a flurry of activity over the next few days, getting Monsieur Deux ready for the dog show. He was exercised, washed, brushed, and polished in every way possible. Our house smelled of shampooed dog for days. Alexandra even shone his toenails and brushed his teeth. At the best of times, Monsieur Deux looked confused, but mostly he looked downright surly about this turn of events."

"Poor Monsieur Deux," said Cornelia. "Did the other dogs get jealous that Deux was getting all of the attention?"

"Heavens, no," said Virginia. "Messieurs Un, Trois, and Quatre observed the activities from the sidelines and seemed very grateful to be there. In fact, I'm sure they got away with all sorts of naughty things while our attention was on Deux."

"Very sagacious of them," complimented Cornelia, admiring their craftiness. Virginia continued.

"Finally, the day of the dog show arrived. Monsieur Deux shone like a new penny in Alexandra's lap as we drove to the event. We pulled up at the big hall where the contest would take place, and hopped out under a big banner proclaiming:

CRUFTS CHAMPION DOG SHOW

Underneath that banner was a smaller one, written in gold print:

CRUFTS WELCOMES HER MAJESTY THE QUEEN

"A mob of photographers idled around outside the front entrance, clearly waiting for the queen and her dog to arrive. They ignored us as we carried Monsieur Deux up the walkway, except for one photographer who pointed at our dog's face and laughed.

"The grooming area was a chaotic mess of dogs and cages and tufts of fur. Many of the dogs looked like they had been shipped in from other planets—some with big squished, wrinkled faces and others with skinny, shaking legs and still others with so much pouffy fur that their bodies were undetectable underneath. Most of the dogs barked in cages or stood on special tables, getting brushed and pampered—but some owners showcased their dogs like jewelry in a store window. One huge, long-limbed white poodle lay arranged on a large Chinese-red silk pillow on top of a table. Crossing its front legs haughtily, the dog tolerated a line of well-wishers and admirers.

"Just as we found our stall for Monsieur Deux, all of the noise in the room hushed to a whisper. The queen's dog had arrived with its handlers.

"I don't know if you've ever seen a corgi, but they're short, pudgy little things—hardly the sort of dog you would describe as regal. It trembled with nervousness as its handlers carried it through the crowd. The royal pen stood right in the front of the room, and the corgi's handlers and groomers in white aprons made a great show of combing the dog's coat.

"'That's the dog to beat,' Gladys said to us. She peered through a pair of old binoculars across the crowded room, assessing Monsieur Deux's rival. 'It'll be a piece of steak,' she added.

"'*What?*' I asked.

"'I meant, it will be a piece of *cake*,' Gladys said quickly, and busied herself with Monsieur Deux's grooming. Two dog owners walked past our stall and snickered when they saw Monsieur Deux sitting there. He looked bloated and uncomfortable, like he'd just eaten a big feast.

"'But we have to get through two contests just to get to compete against the queen's dog,' I said doubtfully.

"'We'll be fine,' said Gladys confidently. 'I have a plan.'

"I looked at her suspiciously. Even though it seemed to be about a thousand degrees in the room, Gladys wore a long overcoat. But before I could ask her about it, the judge called over the loudspeaker for all French bulldogs to come to the show ring.

"Alexandra dragged our dog into the ring, where all of the other French bulldogs lined up like stumpy soldiers. Monsieur Deux was last in the line.

Beatrice, Gladys, and I stood next to the ring in the front row. A judge with a helmet of gray hair and tall boots like stovepipes asked the handlers to take their dogs around the circle so she could examine them. Then the most inexplicable thing happened. Each of the little dogs marched around the ring proudly with its handler, its leash making a taut white line in the air. And then, as soon as it passed in front of us, the dog would suddenly lunge at Gladys, barking and gnashing its teeth! The astonished owner would try unsuccessfully to calm his or her dog, and an even more astounded judge had to dismiss one French bulldog after another for bad behavior.

"She eliminated twelve dogs before it was Monsieur Deux's turn to trot around the ring. He trucked along unenthusiastically next to Alexandra, and then planted himself in front of the judge and belched loudly. The judge looked repulsed. But because Monsieur Deux was the only French bulldog left in the ring, the judge grudgingly declared him Best of Breed and sent him on to the next round of the competition. She was careful not to touch him as she handed a winner's ribbon to a beaming Alexandra. No one in the audience even clapped.

"The same thing happened in the next part of the competition. Something about Gladys sent a Boston terrier, a chow chow, a dalmatian, and thirteen other dogs into a frothing tizzy before Monsieur Deux promenaded around the ring. Even the snobby poodle tried to attack Gladys. It pawed deliriously at the velvet rope in front of Gladys and was swiftly eliminated. Once again, at the end of the round, Monsieur Deux was the only dog who hadn't been disqualified.

"This time, when the judge gave an ungrateful Monsieur Deux a Best of Group trophy, our dog farted rudely and looked in the other direction. The trophy gleamed under the spotlights as Alexandra proudly waved it at us. Gladys grinned back at her. Just then, I noticed an array of small flies buzzing around my plump sister. Beatrice and I looked at each other and shrugged as we swatted the gnats away with our dog show programs.

"Finally, it was time for Monsieur Deux to compete for the Best in Show competition, the big prize. Out of thousands of dogs, only about twelve had made it this far, the queen's corgi among them, of course. An army of groomers fussed around the royal contender, getting it ready for the big moment.

"Suddenly a troop of guards swarmed into the show ring, and a voice over the loudspeaker announced: 'Ladies and gentlemen! Please stand in honor of Her Majesty the queen!'

"Everyone in the room bowed and curtsied as the young queen swept into the arena, and a little orchestra played the British national anthem, 'God Save the Queen.' Her guards ushered her to a throne at the edge of the ring. It was time for the final part of the contest to begin.

"I looked down and realized that Monsieur Deux looked fatter than ever before. Alexandra patted his belly worriedly.

"'We've come so far,' she whispered to us. 'He'll just have to muddle through.'

"We all kissed him for good luck. Then Alexandra heaved him off his grooming table and carted him to his place in the ring. Beatrice, Gladys, and I took our seats at the edge of the ring.

"A huge crowd had assembled around the main ring by this time, and a mob of photographers snapped pictures of the dogs and the queen. Stern as a general, the Best in Show judge stalked out into the ring to begin the proceedings. He paced up and down, appraising each of the dogs. He signaled to the first handler to run his sleek gray Weimaraner in a circle around the ring. It cantered along gracefully, and the audience oohed and aahed.

"Then the dog passed in front of Gladys and bucked up in the air, gnashing its teeth and barking.

"'Disqualified!' the judge cried. 'Remove that dog from the ring at once!'

"A murmur swept through the startled crowd. Once the commotion calmed down, the judge asked the handler of the queen's corgi to step forward, and the dog scampered neatly into the center of the ring. The queen leaned forward on her throne and gazed adoringly at her pet. As it passed in front of her, she clapped politely and smiled.

"But once the corgi neared us, it tried to attack Gladys! It writhed at the end of its leash and snapped its chops. The queen gasped.

"'Hey!' shouted a photographer standing across the ring from us, peering through a long lens at Gladys. Then he threw down his camera, ran up to the judge, and whispered something in his ear. The shocked judge gestured to the queen's guards and pointed at Gladys.

"'Take her away!' he shouted.

"About fifteen guards leaped in our direction and whisked Gladys, Beatrice, and me away from the ring and into a grooming room.

"'All right, lass, hand it over,' one of the guards said to Gladys.

"'I don't know what you're talking about,' Gladys answered innocently. Just then, I noticed that she smelled a little funny.

"'Oh, really,' said the guard. 'We'll see about that.'

"He snapped his fingers and another guard stepped out of the room. He returned with a small, yappy Norfolk terrier. The dog scrambled across the room and leaped up on Gladys, madly pawing the front of her long coat.

"'Gah!' shouted Gladys, trying to push the dog away.

"Just at that moment, a big flat bag fell out from inside her coat. The guards snatched it up and ripped it open, revealing the biggest steak I've ever seen! Beatrice let out a horrified scream. The meat plopped down on the floor and the terrier immediately ravished it.

"Needless to say, we got kicked out of the dog show. The photographers delighted in the latest scandal and snapped photos of us being escorted out of the building by the queen's guards. But the fiasco didn't end there.

"The queen was so outraged that Gladys had tried to tamper with the performance of her beloved pet that she issued a statement saying that Gladys had 'attempted to malign and incapacitate a member of the royal family.' Then she put out a decree stipulating that 'Miss Gladys Somerset is henceforth exiled from the British Isles,' lest she attempt another such feat.

"The only one satisfied by this turn of events was Monsieur Deux. Gladys had secretly fed him so much steak before the show that he couldn't have cared less about the meat hidden in Gladys's coat. Sluggishly delighted to be out of the ring for good, he slept for two whole days while we packed our bags to leave the country."

"What did your parents do when they found out you got in trouble?" Cornelia asked.

"Well, naturally they tried to make us come home right away," said Virginia. "So we did what any reasonable girls would do: we got on a boat to India before they could come over to London to get us."

"I don't know anyone who gets into as much trouble as Gladys," said Cornelia. She thought for a minute. "Well, except for my mother's friend Gunner Joerg."

"Do you mean the pianist Gunner Joerg?" asked Virginia with great interest. "What happened to him?"

"He's always in trouble," said Cornelia. "Once he conflagrated a restaurant with a cigarette. My mother said it was an accident, but he got put in jail anyway."

"Goodness," said Virginia. "I don't think that even Gladys ever set anything on fire. Permanent exile from England was her biggest claim to fame. But see? It sounds like your mother has been telling you stories about colorful people too."

"Once in a while," said Cornelia. "But I like your stories better."

"Why don't you tell some of them to your mother when she gets back from London?" asked Virginia. "It will give you something to talk about."

"It wouldn't be the same," said Cornelia, not wanting to tell Virginia that Lucy knew nothing of their friendship. "She doesn't like words and stories like we do."

Virginia studied Cornelia. "Well, maybe she'd surprise you."

"Maybe," said Cornelia doubtfully.

She thanked Virginia for the tales about England and went home for dinner, her mind filled with thoughts about ghosts, planes, and royal dog shows gone awry.

Chapter Nine

A Different Sort of Play

A month later, Cornelia sat and read in her bedroom armchair on a Sunday afternoon. She had long since memorized the second book of long words that Virginia had given her. On her lap instead lay an old copy of *The Arabian Nights* from Virginia's English library.

As she read about the beautiful Arabian storyteller Scheherazade, Cornelia marveled that she had her own secret Scheherazade next door. She was reading a story about a genie and a merchant when footsteps approached her closed door.

"Madame Desjardins," Cornelia called out, hoping to prevent any long, interfering conversations. "I'm

reading a very important book. No morology this afternoon, please." ("Morology" meant "nonsense" or "mere
foolishness.")

There was a moment of puzzled silence on the other
side of the door, followed by a tentative knock.

"Cornelia? May I come in?"

It was Lucy's voice. Cornelia sat up straight as her
mother stepped in uncertainly.

"Hello, darling," Lucy said, looking around curiously,
as if she hadn't been in the room for a long time.

"Hello," said Cornelia, wondering what was going on.

"I'm sorry to barge in on your afternoon reading,"
Lucy said, walking over to Cornelia's desk lamp and
snapping it on. "I was just out having lunch, and I ran
into Natalie Hunt's mother."

Natalie Hunt was a classmate of Cornelia's. Cornelia
didn't know her well but shyly liked her. She was bookish like Cornelia, and had said enough interesting
things in class to earn Cornelia's silent respect.

Lucy picked up a dictionary from Cornelia's desk
and turned it from left to right, admiring the gold bor-
der on it.

"Anyway," she continued. "Natalie's mother was very
nice, and she asked if you would like to go to their
house tomorrow afternoon to play. Some other girls
from your class will be there as well. I accepted the invitation for you—is that all right?"

Cornelia's heart sank. She hadn't been invited to anyone's house since her afternoon with Lauren Brannigan several months earlier.

"You don't have to go," Lucy said. "But I thought it might be fun for you. And the mother seemed lovely and creative—not like the other dullard parents at your school. I'll bet that Natalie is just as interesting." She looked hopefully at her daughter.

Cornelia didn't want to disappoint Lucy, but the invitation made her nervous. What if Mrs. Hunt was like Lauren's hideous mother and badgered her with questions about Lucy? And what if Natalie turned out to be like Lauren, and who were the other girls?

But then Cornelia thought, *What would Virginia do?* She would have seen it as an opportunity for a little adventure, Cornelia reasoned. After all—even though things always seemed to go wrong for the Somerset sisters, everything always turned out well in the end. How wrong could things go in one afternoon at Natalie Hunt's house, compared to getting kicked out of a whole country like Gladys? Cornelia felt a bit braver, and nodded to her mother.

"Okay," she heard herself say.

The next day after school, Cornelia met Natalie outside their school building. Natalie had two more girls with her, Hannah West and Abby Cohen. They all greeted Cornelia cordially as Mrs. Hunt pulled up in a car to take them to Natalie's house. Cornelia felt queasy as she climbed into the backseat and held her backpack on her lap.

To her surprise, Mrs. Hunt didn't ask Cornelia a thing about Lucy during the entire ride uptown. Cornelia remained wary, however, wondering if the questioning would begin once they were inside the Hunts' home. She began to think of especially confusing words that she could throw at the woman when the interrogation began. But as Cornelia settled into her seat, surrounded by three other girls her age, she imagined that she was Virginia going off on one of her trips with Alexandra, Beatrice, and Gladys. She pretended that Pierre and Ahmed sat in the front seat, driving them through the teeming streets of Marrakech.

A short while later, Cornelia found herself sitting in Natalie's big bedroom, still uninterrogated. The girls threw themselves across Natalie's bed and kicked off their shoes.

"So, what do you guys want to do?" asked Natalie, untying her laces.

Cornelia stood there awkwardly, waiting with dread to hear them vote for karaoke or something equally extroverted.

"Let's put on a talent show," suggested Abby.

"We did that last time," said Natalie.

Hannah dug around in her backpack and pulled out

some sheets of paper. "I've already done all of these, so I'm bored of them," she said. "But I brought them along just in case." They were American Girl play scripts.

"*No,*" said Natalie and Abby together, much to Cornelia's relief. Natalie turned to Cornelia. "What do you want to do?"

The room was quiet as all three girls looked at Cornelia, who almost panicked. Then she had an idea.

"I know a play we can act out," she said tentatively. "But it's a different sort of play. And there are four characters as well—all girls—and lots of scenes. But I don't have a script or anything." She was encouraged by the interested looks the other girls were giving her. "I'd have to tell you the stories." Another long moment of silence followed.

"Sure," said Natalie. "Sounds good." Cornelia's heart pounded gratefully.

As she told them about the adventures of Alexandra, Beatrice, Gladys, and Virginia, the other girls listened attentively. They decided to act out the ghost scenes first, starting with the sultan's palace in Morocco and then the Paris catacombs and King Arthur's ruins in England. Natalie got to be Alexandra, Hannah was Beatrice, and Abby played Gladys. The girls made Abby wear a big shirt and they stuffed it with pillows to make her seem nice and plump. Then they all made matching hats out of construction paper and feathers.

Cornelia, of course, got to be Virginia. Shy at first, she became bolder as she told the stories and acted them out. She could almost hear all of the dogs yapping around her as the girls acted out the ill-fated Crufts Dog Show. Natalie pretended to be the queen of England, and when it was Gladys's big moment with the guards and the steak, Natalie leaped around shrieking, "Off with her head! Off with her head!" just like the Queen of Hearts in *Alice in Wonderland.* Cornelia couldn't believe that her idea had gone over so well.

Mrs. Hunt came in just in time to rescue her pillow-cases from a big pair of flashing scissors, for the girls were going to cut the cases up to make pretend *haiks* for the Moroccan *souk* and bridal scene.

"Time to go home, ladies," she said, prying the scissors from Natalie's hand and surveying the mess of feathers, colored paper, and other props that had been used in the Somerset reenactments. "It's nearly dinner-time," she added, hustling the girls out of the room.

On her way out, Cornelia looked with great surprise at the clock on Natalie's bedside table and saw that it was almost six. Usually on her rare after-school play-dates, she was home by four at the latest. Surprised at how much she'd enjoyed herself, Cornelia leaned back happily in the leather seat of Mrs. Hunt's car as they drove back downtown.

"See you tomorrow!" shouted Natalie from the car

window when Cornelia got out. "You have to come over again next week—and bring more stories!"

Cornelia waved good-bye. If things had gone this well today, Cornelia thought to herself in the elevator, she would soon need more material from Virginia to act out. Cornelia resolved to visit Virginia more than she already did.

The Scheherazade next door now had a demand to meet, and a reputation to uphold.

Madame Desjardins was equally surprised that Cornelia had been gone all afternoon. She left a vat of *vichyssoise* potato and leek soup gurgling on the stove and followed Cornelia upstairs, asking her an onslaught of questions about her time at Natalie's house. Finally, Cornelia told Madame Desjardins that she was suffering from a bout of pnigerophobia ("a dread of being smothered"), which Madame Desjardins assumed was some sort of headache. She brought Cornelia's dinner up to her on a tray that evening. Lucy, as usual, dined out at a restaurant.

Cornelia didn't want to wait until the next day to tell Virginia about her afternoon. After she ate her supper, she made a great show of bringing her backpack into the study and settling down to do her homework.

"I need some privacy," she told Madame Desjardins, and she closed the door. She listened as Madame

Desjardins cleaned the kitchen and then clumped upstairs to watch television. She waited until she heard the canned laughter of an old sitcom upstairs.

Then she quietly opened the door to the study and tiptoed down the hallway, out the front door, and over to Virginia's apartment next door.

Cornelia rang the front bell. No one answered. She impatiently rang again after a minute. Nothing. Cornelia stared in frustration at the blue ATTENTION! CHIEN BIZARRE sign, and silently willed Patel to open the door. After a few more minutes, she gave the bell one last ring, ready to give up. Then she heard footsteps from inside, coming down the stairs.

"Yes?" said Patel, opening the door abruptly. He looked down and saw Cornelia standing there. "Oh, Cornelia," he said.

"Hello, Patel-ji," Cornelia said, brushing past him and into the front foyer. She started to take off her shoes. "I've come for a cup of tea with Virginia," she said.

Patel looked tired and worried. "This evening is not good," he said after a moment. "Virginia cannot have tea with you at this time."

"Oh," said Cornelia.

"She is not well," said Patel, looking up the stairs. "I mean, she is very tired tonight."

"Oh," said Cornelia again, feeling very small and deflated all of the sudden.

"But maybe tomorrow she will feel better," said Patel, trying to sound more buoyant. Cornelia noticed that for the first time in weeks, his hands weren't covered in paint. She glanced up the staircase, half hoping to see Virginia standing at the top of it. Then she put her shoes on again and said good night. She slipped back into her apartment and finished her homework.

After school the next day, she rang their doorbell again. Cornelia was sure that Virginia had rested enough by now, and imagined her sitting at her desk in her English library, tapping away on her old typewriter. But once again, Cornelia had to ring several times before Patel opened the door.

"Good afternoon, Cornelia-ji," he said. He had dark circles under his eyes.

"Is Virginia better?" asked Cornelia, not feeling confident enough today to walk into the foyer. Mister Kinyatta barked from the kitchen.

Patel rubbed his temples with his forefingers as if he had a headache. "I'm afraid she is not," he said. "She is still very weary." He turned around and said, "Shush!" in the direction of the kitchen.

"Cornelia," he said, brightening slightly. "Would you mind taking Mister Kinyatta for a walk? He is cooped up all day in the kitchen."

"Okay," said Cornelia, still disheartened about being

refused admission to tea with Virginia. But the prospect of playing with Mister Kinyatta was a comforting compensation.

She took the dog to the park near their house and let him stump around the bushes and tree trunks. Strong as a little mule, he tugged on his leash as he strained to sniff this branch and inspect that leaf. Every once in a while, he turned back and looked at Cornelia as if wondering why she—and not Virginia or Patel—was at the other end of the leash.

This arrangement went on for the rest of the week. Each day after school, Cornelia stopped by the apartment next door to inquire about Virginia. And each day Patel told Cornelia that Virginia still could not receive guests, and asked her to walk Mister Kinyatta.

Cornelia became confused and worried about why Virginia wouldn't see her. Was Virginia tired of telling Cornelia her stories? Or worse, was she bored by Cornelia's company? Had Cornelia been impolite or said something wrong? She racked her memory, trying to recall if she had done or said something to upset Virginia. She couldn't think of anything, and even began to panic about being cursed. After all, her father was totally indifferent to her and Lucy seemed to need her distance too. And now even Virginia seemed to be losing interest in Cornelia.

But despite all of her dark fears and doubts,

Cornelia always took Mister Kinyatta's leash from Patel and led the dog out of their building. The pair would walk around the neighborhood, sometimes to the park, sometimes to the bakery, and sometimes to the book-store. Once Cornelia took him to Zoomies pet store and bought him a doggie cookie shaped like a crown.

By Friday, the little dog waited for Cornelia by the gate in the kitchen doorway, barking and leaping when he saw her. They were becoming good friends.

"Virginia-ji would like you to join her for tea upstairs," said Patel as he opened the front door the next day.

A flood of relief washed over Cornelia, but uneasi-ness crept into her as she followed Patel up the stairs. Why wasn't Virginia downstairs typing her story? Or spying on neighbors from the French drawing room, or sipping mint tea in the Moroccan forest room? She was about to ask Patel, when they reached a door at the end of the upstairs hallway.

"Here we are," said Patel, opening the door. "Cor-nelia-ji is here to see you," he announced to Virginia inside.

As she stepped into the room, Manhattan seemed to melt away and Cornelia found herself inside what seemed like an ancient temple in India. A scratchy layer of chalky sky-blue paint covered all of the walls, mak-ing the room seem as cool and calm as an indolent, faraway sea. Marble, the color of pale opals, paved the floor. The huge bronze statue of Saraswati, with her crown and instrument, stood facing out an enormous arched window, as if ruling over the Hudson River below.

And as if this weren't lovely enough, a second, cloistered room had been constructed inside the larger room. Each of its four walls had a huge arch carved out of it, and white flowing curtains covered the openings.

"Cornelia, I'm in here," said Virginia's voice from inside the cloister.

Cornelia saw Virginia's silhouette through the filmy drapes. She drew a curtain aside to reveal the writer sitting in a soft white bed with a white gauze canopy cascading over it. Virginia wore a long grass-green silk robe and her hair was tied up in a silk scarf the color of jade.

Cornelia tentatively sat on a white chair next to Virginia's bed. Virginia, already slender to begin with, had lost weight. Her cheekbones jutted out in sharp arcs below the dark areas under her eyes, and the hollows in her cheeks seemed much deeper. A ripple of alarm ran through Cornelia, and she remembered for the first time in months that Virginia was an old lady. A streak of sunlight fell across Virginia's face, making her scarf seem greener than emeralds. Her tired eyes still shone mischievously, which reassured Cornelia ever so slightly.

"Finally, you get to see the Indian room," Virginia said softly. "Isn't it wonderful?"

"It's beautiful," said Cornelia as the peacefulness of the room soothed her. "It feels like summer to me."

Virginia smiled and looked around. "That's how it makes me feel as well. Light as a petal and calm as a still night."

She pulled aside one of the white curtains and gazed through the window at the river. "Even so, the main reason I love this room is because of the view. You know how nosy I am. I like to know everything that's happening around me at all times. From where I'm sitting on this bed, I can see everything that's happening on land, river, and sky—and that is very gratifying."

She turned her attention back to Cornelia. "Patel tells me that you've been taking care of Mister Kinyatta this week. I can't tell you how much we appreciate it. And that dog won't let just *any*body take him for a walk, you know. He clearly adores you."

Virginia's praise took away some of the chill inside Cornelia, but her stomach still tingled nervously. Suddenly she felt the old urge to shield and numb herself with long words.

"Have you been inflicted with a malady?" she asked. "You've been indisposed for nearly a fortnight." This was her way of asking Virginia if she'd been ill for the past week or two.

Virginia paused. "It's true that I haven't been feeling very well," she said, choosing her words carefully. "But today I have more energy. Look."

She pointed to a little table next to her bed. The old black typewriter sat there, with a sheet of white paper wedged into the top. A stack of paper covered in sentences rested next to it.

"The writing has been going *very* well," Virginia told Cornelia. "I've written a whole chapter this afternoon alone."

"That's splendiferous," said Cornelia. "When can I read it?"

"Soon. Have some patience, old girl," smiled Virginia. "Not that *I* have ever had any patience, but it's such easy advice to dispense to someone else."

"Well, can you tell me another story in the meantime?" Cornelia asked impatiently. "I need some new material right away."

"You *need* material?" asked Virginia quizzically. "Why?"

Cornelia took a deep breath. "I made some new friends at school, and the other day, I told them your stories about Morocco and France and England," she said, hoping that Virginia wouldn't mind. "We turned them into plays and acted them out. We even made matching hats and stuffed Abby's clothes full of pillows so she could be Gladys."

"Well," Virginia said, leaning back into her pillows. "I'm honored to be your muse, and delighted to hear that the audacious escapades of the Somerset sisters are passing into legend already. You know that you're someone special when you inspire an art form while you're still alive. And who did you get to play?"

Cornelia blushed. "You," she said, suddenly shy. "You're not mad that I told other people your stories, are you?"

"Of course not!" exclaimed Virginia, sitting up straight as a poker. "They're *meant* to be shared. That's the whole *point* of them. I'm just delighted that you've deemed these girls worthy enough of both your company and the tales. Bravo, Cornelia."

"Will you tell me another story?" pleaded Cornelia. "Could you *please* tell me what you're writing? Please?"

Virginia shook her head. "Not yet," she said. "That one isn't finished yet, and I won't tell a story unless I've determined its end. All story endings should be either witty or meaningful—preferably both."

She paused. "Notice I didn't say that story endings should be tidy, Cornelia," she added solemnly. "Very few stories have tidy endings, or entirely happy ones. But a story can have a positive ending without it being wholly happy. The one that I'm writing now has just that sort of ending. I know that it's going to be sad, but good things will come of the events in it."

"I wish that you would just tell me what it's about," said Cornelia, frustrated. "You've been writing for weeks and won't read anything to me. Patel's been painting for weeks, and he won't show me anything. I thought that you just said stories are supposed to be shared with other people."

"All right, all right," Virginia said, lying back again. "If there's one thing I hate, it's being caught in a contradiction, so I'll offer you this concession. Where's your mother today? I'll tell you a story about whatever country she is in. And then you can surprise her with how much you know about where she's been when she comes home."

"She *is* at home, here in New York," Cornelia said. "For once." She looked around the room. "Will you tell me a story about India instead?"

Virginia closed her eyes for a minute. Cornelia felt a surge of shame about exhausting her friend. "Are you too tired?" she asked guiltily. "Do you want me to come back another day?"

Virginia opened her eyes. "No," she said. "Today is better than tomorrow." She was quiet for a moment. "Okay, I'll tell you about India. That's where I met Patel, remember? And by the way, did you see the paintings in this room?"

Cornelia walked out of the cloister and up to a vertical line of small paintings hanging on one of the walls.

Intricate and brilliantly colored, the images looked like they belonged in a museum, or at the very least, in one of the wonderful old books in Virginia's English library.

"Patel painted those many, many years ago," Virginia called from her bed. "When he was around your age—can you believe it? They're scenes of India's history. Filled with gods and princes, invaders and defenders."

Cornelia stared at them, astonished. The pictures were so fine that she couldn't believe that they'd been done by an eleven-year-old child. She reached out and ran her fingers over them, sure that the vivid reds would be hot to the touch, and the blues cool.

Virginia watched Cornelia's reaction to the pictures and said, "I'm trying to decide what to tell you about, but there are so many stories to choose from! Stories about temples and monsoons, about festivals and ele-phants and rebellions. And, oh! The story about when Gladys became a movie star in Bollywood! That's the In-dian version of Hollywood, by the way."

Virginia grew excited as she talked, but then she fal-tered and seemed to wilt a little bit. She sat back and was quiet. And then she told Cornelia, "It would take me years to tell you everything that I want to. But I have enough energy for only one story today—and this tale means more to me than all of the other ones put to-gether."

Cornelia ran back to her chair next to the bed and

sat down. Virginia's sudden seriousness worried and intrigued her, and she leaned forward to make sure that she heard every word.

Virginia closed her eyes again. "Cornelia, you simply wouldn't *believe* the colors of India," she said.

And the Scheherazade of Greenwich Street began to tell her story.

Chapter Ten

Ɽndia, 1954

"'I've never seen such vibrant colors in my life,' Alexandra said to us as we tore through the streets of Bombay in another rickety old car. So many people and animals filled the streets that every five minutes, our driver had to grind the car to a halt, pitching us into each other's laps. We bumped down a street lined with low houses with bright red roofs.

"'Is that *fruit* up there, drying on the tops of those buildings?' Gladys said. 'Pull over—I want to get some. I'm starving.'

"Our driver laughed. 'Trust me, *memsahib*—you do not want to eat those fruits,' he said. 'You will be very sorry if you do. They are sun-dried chilies, hot enough to start a fire.'

"'Oh,' said Gladys, still eyeing the peppers.

"We careened past a long stall where two ladies were hanging up dyed saris, the bright dresses Indian women wore draped around their bodies. Hanging side by side on a clothesline, the dresses formed a billowing rainbow of greens, blues, pinks, purples, and oranges.

"We had only gotten to India an hour earlier. Like I told you, we ran away from England after Gladys's performance at the dog show. We left Messieurs Un, Deux, Trois, and Quatre with a good friend in London, because the sea journey would have been too hard for four French bulldogs. We promised to come back for them in a few months.

"Now, years before, when our father was at Oxford University, he'd met an Indian prince, a maharaja, who studied at the same college. This prince's name was Nihar Singh, maharaja of Maharashtra. We had never met this prince before, but boldly wrote to him from England and asked if we could visit his grand palace just outside the city. Within a week, we had our reply, written on a long scroll of paper:

> *Dear Somerset sisters,*
>   *I am always delighted to welcome the children of important people to my home. Prepare to be impressed by my majestic presence and splendid palace.*

You shall be treated like royalty.

Yours truly,

Nihar Singh,
Maharaja of Maharashtra

"Naturally, we accepted his hospitable offer. Over the Atlantic Ocean we sailed, through the Strait of Gibraltar into the Mediterranean Sea, through the famous Suez Canal into the Red Sea and then the Indian Ocean and into the Arabian Sea after that—until *finally* we saw the famous Gateway of India shining on the sunny shores of Bombay. Our legs were so shaky from our long sea voyage that we wobbled like newborn colts through the gateway's regal arch. Our driver spotted us easily amidst the hundreds of people at the dock and ferried us off to our new home in Bombay.

"When we got to the outskirts of the city, our car drove along a seemingly endless wall that towered nearly one hundred feet up.

"'What is this?' Beatrice asked the driver. He turned around and grinned at us.

"'This is the wall around His Excellency's palace,' he said.

"'But the wall is at least two miles long!' Beatrice whispered to us in disbelief as the car pulled up to a huge iron gate in the wall. It took five men to heave it open.

"We drove into the estate on a wide driveway paved with pure white pebbles. It wound over vast green lawns and past brilliant gardens and through several small palm forests. Monkeys peered down at us from the tree branches, their black eyes glittering.

"'Are we almost there?' asked Gladys, whose stomach was growling noisily.

"'We have to drive through only five more gates, *memsahib*,' the driver assured us.

"'Five!' we exclaimed together.

"At long last, the palace came into sight, a sprawling mansion made of blinding snow-white marble. A very dark, stern man in a stark white turban waited on the front steps for us. He stood as still as a statue until our driver opened a door for us. Pressing his palms together, he raised his hands in front of his face and bowed slightly.

"'*Namaste. Mera naam Kinyatta hai,*' he said to us in Hindi. 'Good afternoon. Welcome to the home of His Excellency the maharaja of Maharashtra. My name is Kinyatta. I will be attending to you while you are here. Come with me, *kripaya*— please.' And he turned around efficiently and walked out of the hot sun and into the palace."

"So *that's* how Mister Kinyatta got his name?" blurted out Cornelia. "From the man at the palace?"

"Yes, indeed," said Virginia. "I don't know that the real Kinyatta would have appreciated the peculiar homage, but it was my own small way of honoring him. He was such an interesting man. We learned later that he was originally from Africa, not India. When he was a boy, he'd come to India with his parents, and all three became servants in the maharaja's house for many years."

"We followed him into the palace. 'There are more than eight hundred rooms,' Kinyatta informed us. 'You must always have a guide, or I promise that you will get lost. His Excellency has prepared a special banquet in honor of your arrival. He waits now to greet you in his private wing,' he added, and steered us to the part of the palace where the maharaja lived.

"Our expedition through the vast halls and pillared colonnades and gardens was like strolling through an endless enchanted labyrinth. At one point, we heard the trumpeting of an elephant.

"'Yes, the zoo is over there,' said Kinyatta, pointing over a high wall covered in magenta blossoms. 'His Excellency has sixty elephants, and they are very noisy.'

"At last, we approached the doors to the maharaja's personal reception room. Two servants in uniforms and white gloves opened the grand doors for us. The maharaja sat at the far end of the hall on a huge throne. An extensive collection of guns and swords hung on the walls.

"Gladys pinched my arm as we promenaded in. 'Look down there, to the left,' she said under her breath.

"My stomach lurched when I spotted several low tables made out of real elephants' feet! And ahead of us, at the maharaja's feet, a big tiger hide served as a rug on the white marble floor. The tiger's head—fangs and all—was still attached.

"'Come in, come in,' the maharaja laughed. 'He still has teeth, but he cannot bite you anymore.' He stomped across the tiger's back as he came forward to greet us.

"Remembering our manners just in time, we pressed our palms together and said to our host, '*Namaste,* Your Excellency.' Jewels sparkled on the maharaja's fingers and turban, and he spread his arms wide, gesturing to the room around us.

"'I am pleased to welcome the Somerset sisters to my enviable palace, which my ancestors built hundreds of years ago,' he declared. 'And it will belong to my sons and my sons' sons as well. Unless those thieves in the new government get their hands on it,' he added darkly. 'But never mind that now. It is time for the banquet that I am hosting in honor of the importance of your father.'

"'That's very . . . kind of you, Your Excellency,' said Alexandra.

"'Yes, well, he is a great man,' said the maharaja. "My heart bleeds for him that he has no sons to make him proud. Ah, well, you will all just have to marry good husbands.'

"Gladys raised an eyebrow at me as we followed the prince to another set of closed doors, which were immediately whipped open by more servants.

The maharaja swept into a large dining hall next door. When we tiptoed in after him, nearly a hundred people sitting in the room stood up and bowed slightly. The maharaja had invited all of the other maharajas from the Maharashtra region to dine with us. He clapped his hands and announced, 'I would like to introduce the daughters of the Honorable Augustus Somerset of New York City. He is the *very* important president of a bank and an old friend from Oxford. May his daughters serve him well.'

"All of the men in the room murmured in agreement. Beatrice coughed indignantly.

"We sat with him at table on a canopied stage at the front of the room. Servants set down heavy crystal bowls filled with water, floating candles, and rose petals in front of us. The twins sat to the left of the maharaja, and Gladys and I to the right. Each sister had a little throne, and of course, the maharaja had the biggest throne of all. Waiters brought in the feast and served it to us on plates of solid gold.

"'I have planned many events to entertain you,' the maharaja told us as he sucked on a big chicken bone. 'Tomorrow, I'm playing in a polo match, giving you the chance to watch and clap as we thunder gallantly by on our horses. The day after that, there is another banquet at Maharaja Rajiv Azmi's palace. And the day after that, we will go on a grand hunt and shoot tigers, so you can bring home the hides as a gift for your father.'

"'We would like to tour Bombay as well, Your Excellency,' Alexandra piped up, 'and see the markets and buildings and daily life as well.'

"Suddenly every guest in the room dropped his gold knife and fork and stared at her. The maharaja put down his own fork and said, 'I beg your pardon?'

"Alexandra's face reddened. 'I said . . . uh . . . that we would like to see daily life in the city as well,' she stammered. 'The markets and—I don't know— how other people in India live. The ones who don't live in palaces.'

"The maharaja glared at her. 'Why would you want to do that?' he demanded. The servants had stopped in their tracks and stood like statues.

"'It's just that we've never been here before,' Alexandra said in a small voice. 'We want to get to know the country.'

"'Well,' the maharaja snorted disapprovingly. He began eating again. The rest of the princes, taking the cue from their host, picked up their gold cutlery and resumed the feast. The servants scurried among the grand tables again as well, attending to the guests.

"'Such a thing is easily arranged,' the maharaja said. 'Kinyatta can give you a motor tour around the city tomorrow, before the polo match.'

"As you can imagine, none of this was going over well with Gladys, although she was clearly enjoying the cuisine.

"'We had a motor tour this morning, on our way

to the palace,' she said, her mouth full of *Malvani kombdi,* chicken in coconut sauce. 'What my sister means, Mr. Maharaja, is that we would like to actually get *out* of the car and prance about a little bit. Get to know some of the people in town. Local color and whatnot. We've been around, you know. We can handle it.' She took another big bite of chicken and gave an exaggerated wink to the maharaja, who looked appalled.

"'Maybe it's a good idea if you do not attend the polo match tomorrow, after all,' the prince said disdainfully as he peered around, hoping that none of the other princes had overheard her remarks.

"'Kinyatta!' he exclaimed. The African servant stepped forward from the wall, where he'd been standing silently with his hands behind his back. 'Take the Somerset sisters on a tour of the city tomorrow,' the maharaja commanded. 'You will be responsible for their welfare and for protecting them from the undesirable elements of the urban populace. And there are *many* of those, ladies. Enjoy your little outing.' He leaned in over his plate and sawed a piece of lamb with his fork and knife. Kinyatta nodded once and took his place at the wall again.

"The maharaja ignored us for the rest of the feast, which lasted for eleven more courses. The four of us practically ran out of the banquet hall when it was over. Kinyatta led us to a set of rooms around a private courtyard.

"The blue Indian moonlight filtered into my

room through latticed windows, casting shimmering curves and shapes on the pale floor. I fell gratefully into my huge, silk-covered feather bed and dreamed about being hunted by tigers."

"I would have hated to sit near the maharaja," said Cornelia. "The way he keeps talking about your dad reminds me of how people always act around me. I'm never just Cornelia. Instead, I'm always 'Lucy's daughter,' and it drives me crazy."

"It was infuriating, I agree," said Virginia. "And it was a lot worse in those days, and more so in certain cultures. For the first part of their lives, girls were seen as property of their fathers, and later, their husbands. I loved my father, but I certainly didn't enjoy being seen solely as his personal possession by other people. None of the Somerset sisters did. Like I told you when I first met you, that's one of the main reasons none of us ever got married."

"I hope you taught the maharaja a lesson," said Cornelia. "Like Alexandra and Beatrice did to the famous artist in Paris."

"You'll hear how we dealt with him," answered Virginia.

"The next morning, Kinyatta collected us after breakfast and led us through the palace out to a waiting car. A driver took us back past the gardens and over the lawns and through the six guarded gates and finally out onto the street again. An hour later, we rode into the center of Bombay.

"We strolled through the crowded streets, dodging bicycles and donkeys and even cows among the throngs of people. An aching, majestic beauty filled the city and its ancient and colonial buildings. However, we found it difficult to admire the arches and minarets because fleets of beggars besieged us everywhere we went.

"I know that you're used to seeing homeless people here in New York City, Cornelia, but *nothing* would prepare you for what it's like in India. I've never seen such poverty. Some of the beggars were very old and some carried babies and some of them were just barely older than babies themselves. Guilt and pity gnawed at my heart, and I began to lose interest in sightseeing. It just seemed like a frivolous pastime.

"Kinyatta took us to the Crawford Market inside a big building with a famous clock tower on top. The market reminded me of the *souks* in Morocco with their thousands of stalls filled with fruit and flowers in every imaginable color. Great lanterns shaped like flying dragons dangled from the ceiling above.

"Yet once again, beggars thronged around us immediately. Kinyatta shouted unsuccessfully at them to leave us alone. Alexandra and Beatrice emptied their pockets of coins and gave them to several barefoot children who trailed us around the stalls. Within minutes, we were like the Pied Piper of Hamelin, with dozens of poor children following us and tugging on our skirts. When we got out of the market into the harsh midday sunshine, Kinyatta shooed them away from us.

"'You will never be able to give something to everyone,' he told us. 'It is best not to give them hope. Let us go back to His Excellency's palace now.'

"But good old Gladys, as usual, had a guide-book.

"'I'm not ready to go back to that old blowhard's house yet,' she declared. 'It says here on page 147 that there's a market nearby called the Thieves' Market. Now, that sounds exciting to me. I've always wanted to learn how to steal something. Let's go learn from the professionals.' She clumped down the street.

"'Gladys-ji,' Kinyatta called after her. 'There will be more beggars than ever there. Let us go back. His Excellency will be expecting you.' But Gladys didn't pay any attention, so we had no choice but to follow her down to the Thieves' Market.

"Kinyatta was right—we saw many beggars and no thieves. Within minutes, children in rags surrounded us, begging for money. Beatrice opened her pockets to show them that she had no more coins to give them. After ten more minutes of this, she burst into tears and we turned to leave.

"Then something caught Alexandra's attention. She strode over to a ramshackle tin shack. 'Beatrice, come here,' she said excitedly. 'I want you to see something.'

"We all ran over to the stall. Several paintings on flat wood boards were propped up against its outside wall. A young Indian boy, about eleven years old, sat on the ground next to them. He looked up at us hopefully.

"'These are fantastic,' Beatrice said. 'Where did they come from?' she asked the boy, who didn't answer her.

"'He does not understand English,' Kinyatta said, and translated Beatrice's question to the boy, who responded timidly in Hindi. He looked slowly from Kinyatta to each of us, staring into our eyes. Kinyatta looked at the child suspiciously.

"'He says he is an orphan,' Kinyatta reported. 'His father was a painter and left behind the paints when he died. The boy claims he painted the pictures here himself, and he is trying to sell them to buy food.' He frowned, and added, 'I do not believe him. The pictures are too good. I think he steals them from somewhere. Anyway, he is Harijan. Let us go back to the palace.'

"'He's what?' I asked.

"'Harijan,' repeated Kinyatta patiently. 'An untouchable.'

"'What does that mean?' asked Gladys indignantly.

"Kinyatta sighed. 'Nearly everyone in India be-
longs to a group called a caste. In one caste, you
have the princes and warriors and they are called
the Kshatriyas. The merchants' and businessmen's
caste is called the Vaisyas. And so on. And then people who have no caste are called the untouchables.
They are not allowed to be near the people from
other castes. This boy is a polluted untouchable. Do
not go near him or his stolen paintings. His Excellency would be angry.'

"My heart nearly broke as I looked down at the
dirty boy, who was barefoot and pitifully thin. 'What
has he done to become an untouchable?' I asked.

"'Nothing,' said Kinyatta. 'That's just the way he
was born. The system has been in place for hundreds of years.'

"'Sounds like a pretty cruel system to me,' I
said. I bent down and pointed at the boy's hands.
'Look at his fingernails! They're caked with colors,
like Alexandra's and Beatrice's when they paint. I
know an artist's hands when I see them. He didn't
steal these pictures. He's an incredibly talented boy,
and he doesn't have a fighting chance in this city, because of the so-called system.'

"I leaned in toward him. 'What's your name?' I
asked him. Kinyatta repeated my question in Hindi:
'Aapka naam kya hai?'

"'*Mera naam Patel hai,*' answered the little boy
cautiously.

"'*Mera naam Virginia hai,*' I said. 'Kinyatta,

please tell Patel that I'd like to buy all of his paintings, and that I would like him to paint me another one,' I said. 'We'll come back to get it when he's done.'

"'Virginia-ji,' Kinyatta said, greatly troubled. 'You cannot bring the art of an untouchable into the palace of His Excellency. He would be outraged.'

"'Why not?' asked Gladys. 'Mr. Maharaja doesn't have to know, and you can keep a secret—can't you, Kinyatta, old pal? Why should we let this kid starve, just because your boss is a conceited snob and has half a dozen gates around his palace to shut the world out?'

"A funny look came over Kinyatta's face. After a minute, he stepped forward and spoke with Patel. The boy stacked the pictures up, tied them with a long strand of dirty string, and placed them at Kinyatta's feet.

"'He says that he will have another painting for you in three evenings from now,' said Kinyatta. 'If we come back here, he will be waiting for us.'

"I dug all of the money out of my purse and gave it to Patel, who took it timidly.

"'Tell him that we'll be here,' I said. 'What else did he say?'

"Kinyatta swallowed. 'It is hard to translate exactly,' he answered. '*Chalo,*' he added, which meant 'Let's go.' He turned and walked away.

"The boy watched us as we walked away. Later that afternoon, we smuggled the Harijan's paintings through the six gates of the maharaja's palace and hid them in Alexandra's room."

"What did the pictures look like?" asked Cornelia. She could hardly believe that the elegant man downstairs had once been a bereft orphan in the Bombay Thieves' Market.

"They were the pictures that you just looked at on the wall," answered Virginia. "Can you imagine coming across such things propped up in the dirt against a shack, only to realize that a street boy had done them? Patel was a startling child prodigy." The word "prodigy" meant "a person with exceptional talents."

"My mother was a child prodigy too," said Cornelia. "She played her first concert at Carnegie Hall when she was thirteen years old. People remind me of that all the time, and then they ask me when I'll be giving *my* first concert."

Virginia paused. "I hate to probe, Cornelia, but I always *have* been curious why you don't play the piano too," she said.

Like a seashell snapping shut, Cornelia went silent. Finally, looking at her lap, she answered in a quiet voice, "Because I don't want to be compared to my mother all the time, and I don't love music like she does. I like listening to it, but I like reading better. Nobody ever understands that, and I always get told that I should want to be a famous pianist like her and my dad. Sometimes I wish I'd been born without fingers so no one would ask me that anymore."

This was one of the longest speeches she had ever made in front of Virginia, who nodded sympathetically.

"Well, everyone has different dreams and talents," she said carefully. "And I respect your reasons. You're a strong-willed girl, Cornelia, who knows her own mind. I am always inspired by the incredible resources of children like you and Patel when he was your age."

Cornelia relaxed in her chair. Virginia really was miraculous. No other adult had ever treated her with such consideration and respect. She looked up from her hands and at the face of her tired friend.

"Did the maharaja find out about Patel's paintings?" she asked, eager to hear the end of the story before Virginia got too weary to tell it. "And what happened when you went back to the market?"

"Ah, now we're getting to my favorite part of the story," said Virginia.

"The next day, Kinyatta served us tea and *bebinca* cakes in our courtyard at teatime. Gladys had just polished off the last cake when the maharaja strode into the quad, attended by a gaggle of servants.

"We all greeted him from our table under a grove of orange trees: '*Namaste*, Your Excellency.'

"The maharaja looked imperiously down at us. 'How was the Somerset excursion into town?' he asked. 'How was Real Daily Life? You act as though you are missionaries, not heiresses.'

"'We should have listened to you in the first place, Your Excellency,' I said quickly. 'All of the beggars—it was just repulsive. You were absolutely right.'

"The maharaja's face registered surprise at this apparent change of attitude. 'Well!' he sputtered, and collected himself. 'I *always* am. I'm pleased that you came to your senses. In any case, you missed a fine polo match,' he said, and sat down with us. 'I was most impressive. I am sorry that you were not there to enjoy it.'

"Several monkeys ran across the patio, screeching as they went.

"'I couldn't help but notice your wonderful art collection throughout the palace,' Gladys said, changing the subject. 'You have such divine paintings.'

"'Yes,' agreed the maharaja. 'It is true that I have supremely good taste. I buy paintings from only the most important artists and galleries around the world. Just like my father and grandfather and great-grandfather before me. Our art collection is the envy of all India.'

"Alexandra cocked an eyebrow as she sipped from her teacup. 'Your Excellency,' she said, 'did you know that Beatrice and I studied with one of the most famous artists in the world, Monsieur Pablo Picasso?'

"'Is that so!' said the maharaja, his interest tweaked at hearing such a legendary name uttered in his own courtyard.

"'Yes, it is,' said Beatrice. 'And, well, we would

like to offer you a gift for your art collection: one of our own paintings to thank you for the gracious hospitality you've shown us.'

"'I am most interested to see this gift,' replied the maharaja, smoothing his silk shirt down over his fat stomach. The jewels pinned to his turban twinkled in the afternoon sunlight.

"'Very good!' exclaimed Alexandra. 'I'll just run to my room now to get it. Wait here!'

"Five minutes later, she returned with a painting. 'Here it is, Your Excellency,' she said, plunking it down against the table.

"The maharaja drew in his breath sharply. 'How captivating!' he said, getting up and examining the painting closely. 'It is most original! Yes, yes—I can definitely see the influence of the great Monsieur Picasso in your work. And how interesting that it is on a wooden board and not a canvas.' Alexandra and Beatrice looked at the floor modestly. The maharaja continued his inspection. 'I daresay that it is genius!'

"My sisters and I looked slyly at each other.

"'We're honored that Your Excellency has such a high opinion of our humble work,' said Alexandra. 'Please note the texture of the paint. We believe that a work should be pleasant to the touch as well as nice to look at. It's the latest fashion—all the rage in Paris.'

"The maharaja immediately ran his fingers over the thick ridges of paint on the picture. 'Yes, yes—most unusual,' he cried. 'What a fascinating concept! A painting that appeals to two senses instead of just one! I am certainly the first to have such a thing here in India. The other maharajas will be *mad* with jealousy. I will hang it among my most important paintings in the main reception hall!'

"'Maybe we should tell him that it's edible too, just to watch him chomp on it,' Gladys whispered to me as the maharaja's servants carted the painting away.

"The very next day, the maharaja's servants hung the painting between a painting by the famous artist El Greco and another by the great painter Rubens. He threw another lavish party to celebrate his new acquisition, and invited all of his friends over to admire and praise it. All of the princes touched the paint and coveted the maharaja's new possession. One of the guests even begged Beatrice and Alexandra to paint one for his collection as well.

"Of course, Alexandra and Beatrice had *not* painted the now prominently featured gift in the maharaja's gallery—Patel the Harijan did. My sisters and I deliberated for hours about whether we should tell the maharaja the truth about the painting. In the end, we decided against it. We liked the idea of the painting living forever among the maharaja's most treasured items. If the prince ever learned the real identity of the artist, he would burn the picture on a bonfire, and the work was simply too good to sacrifice like that.

"A couple of days later, when we finished our stay at the palace, we negotiated with the maharaja to hire Kinyatta to be our guide all over India. The five of us drove away through the palace grounds, back through the gates, and into Bombay. We made one last stop on our way to the train, which would take us to another city.

"Patel waited for us next to the tin shack in the Thieves' Market. A glistening new painting was by his side. I signaled to Kinyatta, who got out of the car and spoke to the boy.

"'What's Kinyatta saying to Patel?' Alexandra asked, confused about why it was taking so long to buy the painting.

"'He's asking him if he'd like to come with us,' I said, looking at the scene through the window.

"For once, my sisters were stunned into silence. 'Don't worry—if he says yes, I'll take care of him, unless you and Beatrice want to give him painting lessons as well,' I added.

"'Virginia, have you thought this through?' Beatrice said nervously. 'Taking care of a little boy is a huge responsibility, something you know nothing about. And we've only just begun our trip throughout India. We're going to see a *lot* of poor children. You won't be able to take care of all of them, you know.'

"'I know that already,' I said. 'But for some reason, I feel like this boy is *meant* to come with us.'

"Kinyatta clapped his hand on Patel's shoulder,

and they headed toward the car together. The boy climbed happily into the backseat with us and smiled. The only possessions he had with him were the outgrown clothes he wore, his paints, and the painting on his lap.

"And that's how Patel became part of the Somerset coterie. He traveled with us all over India, and then all over the world. We taught him English and he taught us Hindi, and he ended up giving Alexandra and Beatrice painting lessons instead of the other way around. Over the years, he has become my best friend and constant companion."

"Sometimes, when I imagine what might have happened to Patel if Gladys hadn't insisted on going to the Thieves' Market that afternoon over fifty years ago, my heart stops for a moment," said Virginia. "We never would have known each other."

"I guess it was fate," suggested Cornelia.

"Yes, I think it was," said Virginia. "I genuinely believe that some people are *destined* to come into your life. Don't you agree?"

"Do you think that I was destined to meet you?" asked Cornelia.

"Why, certainly," said Virginia. "As the great painter Jackson Pollock supposedly said, 'I deny the accident.' Everything happens for a reason."

The light filtering through the arched window grew dim, and Cornelia was suddenly aware of how long her stay had been.

"I simply *must* take a nap now, Cornelia," Virginia said sleepily. "I wonder if I'll dream about tigers, like I did at the maharaja's palace."

And she closed her eyes.

Chapter Eleven

Tulips in Every Color

Springtime surprised everyone in New York City. It rushed in like an unexpected guest, bearing gifts and good news from faraway places. Sunshine warmed the streets. Crocuses and daffodils pushed their way up through the dirt around the trees lining the streets in Cornelia's neighborhood. The breeze coming off the Hudson River became pleasant and soft. Madame Desjardins opened some of the windows in the living room, study, and music room. At times, the warm spring wind mixed with the light sound of Lucy practicing Mozart on the piano, making the apartment seem more alive than ever before.

Cornelia could not remember a lovelier April. After school, she spent a great deal of time outdoors, watching the city come to life again after the long, cold winter. Every day, she stopped by Virginia's apartment to retrieve Mister Kinyatta, and they trotted up and down Bleecker Street together.

Sometimes Natalie Hunt came over in the afternoons, and the two of them played with Mister Kinyatta in the park. Natalie was the only person whom Cornelia had told about Virginia, and Natalie had sworn to keep Cornelia's friend a secret. The girls spent time talking about Virginia's stories, and even making up their own Somerset tales.

Having a new friend and a dog to play with made Cornelia happy. Her gnawing loneliness slowly disappeared as the days grew longer and warmer. However, she increasingly worried about the person who had changed her lonesome life in the first place. Virginia never came downstairs to her English library, French drawing room, or Moroccan forest room anymore. Whenever Cornelia came to visit, Patel invariably brought her upstairs to the Indian bedroom, where Virginia would be reading or dozing in her cloistered white bed.

And more and more frequently, Patel didn't allow Cornelia upstairs at all and asked her to come back another day. Cornelia tried not to worry, but there was a dark shadow of anxiousness growing in the back of her mind. She desperately wanted Virginia to feel better, come downstairs, and reign over the wonderful kingdom she had built for herself in the apartment behind the blue ATTENTION! CHIEN BIZARRE sign.

It was a sunny Tuesday afternoon, and Cornelia had been saving her allowance for two weeks. She planned to buy Virginia the perfect present on her way home from school. She walked past the Magnolia Bakery and the Biography Bookshop and headed for one of the outdoor flower stalls. A few minutes later, she stood in front of dozens of buckets of fresh tulips. Their red, yellow, and orange petals reminded Cornelia of the saris hanging on the clothesline in India. She breathed in the crisp, fresh scent of the flowers as she picked out a few tulips in every color. Her finished bouquet was as vivid as one of Patel's paintings, and she hoped it would remind Virginia of the Somerset adventure in Bombay.

Walter greeted Cornelia as she walked into her lobby with the present. "Miss Cornelia," he exclaimed in a loud voice. "Right kind of you—who told you it was m' birthday?"

It wasn't his birthday, really—he was just teasing Cornelia. She smiled and gave him a big, fat cherry-colored tulip, and then ran into the elevator.

When she got out of the elevator on her floor, she noticed that the front door to Virginia's apartment was open a crack. *How strange,* she thought to herself. She knocked softly, and when she got no answer, she pushed the door open a little bit.

"Hello?" she called quietly, not wanting to disturb Virginia if she was asleep upstairs. "Patel?"

She walked into the foyer and peeked into the kitchen, expecting to see Mister Kinyatta waiting there. But the room was empty, and the collar and leash weren't on their usual hook on the wall. For some reason, Patel must have taken the dog out this afternoon. She walked back out into the front foyer, sat politely on a chair, and waited for Patel to return.

Then she heard voices murmuring from the Indian bedroom upstairs. Cornelia strained her ears to listen. It sounded as though Virginia was speaking with another lady. Therefore, Virginia was clearly receiving visitors today after all, Cornelia concluded, and she stood up. She worried that her flowers would wilt before she had a chance to show them to Virginia. Then she paused. Would Patel be angry with her if she went upstairs without being announced first? She deliberated for a moment. She finally decided to take her chances, and tiptoed up the staircase.

Cornelia walked down the long hallway to Virginia's bedroom and knocked on the door. The voices inside stopped talking.

"Patel?" Virginia called out weakly from inside.

"It's me, Cornelia," said Cornelia. "I've brought you a present."

She pushed the door open a little bit and peeked inside. Honey-thick, golden afternoon sunlight filled the room. She walked in timidly and approached Virginia's cloistered bed. The lady visitor pulled aside one of the white curtains, and when Cornelia saw who Virginia's guest was, her heart skipped a beat and her stomach turned to water.

It was Lucy.

She sat in the white chair next to the bed, and her eyes were wet from crying. Virginia leaned back in her big white bed, looking very gaunt and serious, her hair wrapped in a silk scarf of the palest pink.

Lucy sat up straight and took a deep breath. "Oh, hello, darling," she said to Cornelia, dabbing at her eyes quickly with her sleeve. "Virginia and I were just having tea and looking at the river. Come over here and show us what you've brought with you."

The sky tumbled down on Cornelia. Tears welled up in her eyes and she clenched the stems of the flowers in her hand. Her heart pounded in her ears as she walked stiffly toward the bed.

"Are those really for *me*?" Virginia asked graciously about the flowers. "They're resplendent, Cornelia. How wonderfully thoughtful of you." She clearly sensed

Cornelia's shocked dismay at finding Lucy sitting there in the white seat where Cornelia herself usually sat.

Lucy stood up. "The tulips *are* lovely," she said. She smoothed down her hair and exhaled slowly. "Virginia is very tired this afternoon, darling. Will you leave the flowers with Patel and come home with me?"

Despair coursed through Cornelia, as though her mother had snooped through a diary in which Cornelia had recorded her deepest secrets. How had this meeting happened? Had Lucy asked Walter about the Somerset sister in the building after all, and simply come by to visit out of curiosity? Or had Madame Desjardins secretly seen Cornelia go next door and told Lucy? In any case, the curtain had fallen.

Lucy turned toward Virginia and took her hand. "I can't tell you how important this talk was for me," she said. "I can tell that you mean a great deal to Cornelia. And I have been such a fan of your writing for so long. I know that I have met a very great lady here today."

Virginia smiled at Lucy. "And I have been an admirer of your music as well," she said. "I hope to hear more Chopin and Rachmaninoff through this wall soon."

As this exchange took place, a sullen rage began to well up inside Cornelia. This was exactly what she had imagined would happen if Lucy ever met Virginia. As of this moment, she was no longer Cornelia S.

Englehart. She was back to being the daughter of Lucille Englehart, Famous Concert Pianist. And all it had taken was one hour and two cups of tea. Cornelia knew that her enchanted confidence with Virginia was over. She could no longer consider the fanciful rooms of Virginia's apartment a hidden, private refuge. She suddenly envisioned Madame Desjardins knocking noisily on the front door, pushing past Patel, barging into the library, and interrupting Virginia while she was telling Cornelia a story. Cornelia supposed that this image was a horrifying glimpse into the future.

"Good-bye," said Lucy, shaking Virginia's hand with great feeling. She put her hand on Cornelia's shoulder and gently steered her toward the bedroom door.

"Cornelia S. Englehart," said Virginia faintly from across the room. Cornelia stopped and looked back at her despondently. "I *love* the flowers. I haven't seen such colors since I was in India with Alexandra, Beatrice, and Gladys."

Cornelia was afraid that she would burst into tears if she said anything, so she kept quiet. But at least Virginia had understood about the tulips.

Patel returned with Mister Kinyatta just as Cornelia and Lucy were leaving. The dog leaped up and down in excitement when he saw Cornelia, who patted him miserably and gave the flowers to Patel to put in a vase.

When the front door to Virginia's apartment closed behind them, Cornelia knew that she would never see the inside of Virginia's home in the same way again.

As soon as they got into their apartment, Cornelia ran upstairs to her bedroom. She slammed her door shut and threw herself down into her armchair. She stared resentfully at her bookshelves for some time, darkly assessing the unfortunate events of the afternoon. The lights in the buildings outside her bedroom window came on one by one as twilight faded into nighttime.

Engrossed in her turbulent thoughts, she didn't even hear Lucy knock on her door. A shaft of light fell across Cornelia's face as the door to her room opened.

"Cornelia Street," Lucy said softly. "I need to talk to you."

Cornelia just looked coldly at her mother from her chair. Lucy came into the dark room and turned on the lamp near Cornelia's bed. The yellow light shone softly on Lucy's austere, often-photographed features.

"Cornelia," Lucy said, sitting on the edge of the bed. "I don't want you to think that I was spying on you by having tea with Virginia this afternoon. I didn't even know she lived next door until this morning. She sent me a note, asking me to come by and talk with her."

This information made Cornelia feel even worse, as though Virginia had betrayed her somehow. And then she remembered that she had never actually *told* Virginia that she was keeping their friendship a secret from Lucy. For now, Cornelia remained silent.

"I didn't know that you had been visiting with Virginia so much," Lucy continued hesitantly. She seemed at a loss for words, and struggled on. "I didn't realize that you were interested in spending time with a grown-up at all. Although Virginia is admittedly more fascinating than most of the adults I hang around with."

Cornelia couldn't control herself anymore. "You've ruined everything!" she shouted. "Virginia was my best friend! She's the only one who ever talked to me and told me stories. She was the only person who ever treated me like I was my own person, and not just your stupid daughter. First my father leaves and never comes back, and now Virginia's gone forever too! And it's all your fault." Hot tears spilled down her cheeks.

Lucy was completely taken aback. She reached out for Cornelia's hand. Cornelia snatched it away.

"Cornelia, listen to me," said Lucy. "Just because I met Virginia doesn't mean that your friendship with her is suddenly going to disappear. She obviously adores you. And it doesn't mean that I'm trying to steal or chase her away from you. But, darling, there's something else that I need to tell you."

Cornelia tucked her chin into her chest. "What?" she said tersely into her shirt.

Lucy got up and kneeled in front of Cornelia's chair. She took Cornelia's hands in her own. As upset as Cornelia was, Lucy's rare display of tenderness startled her.

"Virginia is an amazing woman," Lucy said. "She has lived in many incredible places and known many extraordinary people. And you know better than anyone that she's had more adventures than most people dream about in their whole lives."

She paused and squeezed Cornelia's hands.

"There is simply no easy way to say this, Cornelia," she continued. "Virginia is very sick. She has cancer. And she won't be with us for much longer. She has come back to New York to think about her long, colorful life, and to be close to her memories before she goes."

For Cornelia, the hands of every clock around the world had just stopped. Every bird in the sky froze, wings spread wide. The Hudson River and all of the tugboats in it came to a standstill. She tried to breathe and found that she couldn't. Lucy reached up to smooth Cornelia's hair, and Cornelia didn't even feel her mother's fingers.

Lucy edged Cornelia over on the big armchair and squeezed in next to her, wrapping her arms around her daughter.

"I'm so sorry, darling," she whispered into Cornelia's hair, and rocked her a little bit. "And I'm so sorry that I haven't been here more for you. I just have never wanted to impose my life on yours. I don't want you to be followed around by packs of hungry photographers and get dragged all over this huge, lonely world for concerts. That's what my life was like when I was your age and I hated it. And ever since you were a baby, I've tried to protect you from that life."

She was quiet for a minute. "And I know how hard it's been for you to grow up without a daddy. But I didn't realize how truly lonesome and upset you were and how much you needed your mother around you. Until I talked to Virginia this afternoon."

Cornelia burst into real tears now, deep, convulsing sobs. Lucy hugged her closer and rocked her some more. "It's going to be all right, darling," Lucy told Cornelia over and over again. "I'm here now," she murmured. Cornelia just sat there limply and cried, curling up in her mother's arms for the first time in many years.

Cornelia woke up with a start the next morning, surprised to find her room filled with daylight. Usually it was just getting light when she got up for school. She looked out the window, and the river gleamed like a mirror in the sunshine. Confused, she lay back and tried to remember if it was Saturday already. Hadn't yesterday been Tuesday? Then she remembered the conversation she'd had with Lucy the evening before, and a current of distress ran through her. She got up and went downstairs to see what was going on.

Madame Desjardins wasn't in the kitchen when Cornelia walked in. The housekeeper had left a box of cereal and a bowl on the table, for which Cornelia had no appetite. She looked at the kitchen clock. It was eleven in the morning. She heard Lucy tinkering away at the piano several rooms away.

Cornelia tiptoed up the hallway and listened at the closed door of the piano room. She thought that she recognized the music that Lucy was playing, but she couldn't place it at first. Then she realized that it was the same Mozart sonata that Virginia sometimes played on her record player. It was strange to hear the song without the pops and scratches of the old phonograph. Cornelia silently went upstairs and got dressed. And then she walked out of her apartment and stood in front of Virginia's front door.

She looked at the door for a long time, remembering the first time she'd walked past it and puzzled over the blue sign. She laughed to herself when she thought about Patel scrambling around and chasing after Mister Kinyatta in that very hallway. In her mind, she saw Virginia perched on her Moroccan daybed, surrounded by silk pillows and shaded by palm trees. She thought about all of the black-and-white photos of Alexandra, Beatrice, Gladys, and Virginia in each of the rooms.

She reached out and rang the doorbell.

Patel answered the door quickly for the first time in

weeks. "Ah, Cornelia-ji," he said. "You are here just in time, as usual. I need you to help me carry some things up to Virginia."

Cornelia followed him into the kitchen. Patel ran around the room, piling a silver tray high with teacups, biscuits, sugar, and milk. Finally, he clattered a hot silver teapot into the center of the tray. Cornelia looked at him doubtfully.

"I think it might be too heavy for me," she said apologetically.

"No, no, no," said Patel. "I will carry this. You carry that."

He pointed to a small, battered old leather suitcase. Cornelia recognized it as the case containing the phonograph. "It is heavy too, but you are strong," Patel added. He bustled out of the kitchen with the tray.

The Indian bedroom was bright with midday light. Virginia was sleeping lightly in her big white bed when Patel and Cornelia came into the room. Patel delicately placed the silver tea tray on a table near the bed and Cornelia set the phonograph case down near the window. She and Patel quietly set up the record player and put an old record onto the turntable.

Virginia stirred and opened her eyes when the first strands of music came through the phonograph's old horn. She looked confused for a second, and then smiled. "I almost forgot that I was in New York for a minute," she said. "I thought that we were back in India, Patel."

Patel nodded. He looked at the ceiling as if he was trying to keep from crying. Then he left the room, closing the door behind him.

Virginia watched him go and then looked at Cornelia. She waved her hand gracefully toward the white chair next to her bed. "Please be seated," she said.

Cornelia sat down on her small throne. The tea steamed up from its silver pot.

"Isn't it Wednesday?" Virginia asked Cornelia after a moment of silence. "Why aren't you in school?"

"I don't know," Cornelia replied honestly. "I woke up late, and now here I am." It was quiet again.

Virginia arranged the white covers around her. "Look over there, Cornelia S.," she said, pointing to the windowsill. Cornelia turned around and saw her colorful bouquet, gleaming in a crystal vase in the sunshine. It looked beautiful.

"Virginia," Cornelia said tentatively, still feeling as tender as a bruise from her talk with Lucy the night before. "Why did you invite my mother over to tea yesterday?"

"So I could speak with her about you," Virginia said frankly. "About how extraordinary you are. Everyone is always telling you how extraordinary *she* is, which is true. And now it's time for Lucy to start hearing the same about you."

Cornelia looked down, both flattered and flustered. She didn't say anything.

"Cornelia," Virginia said softly. "Your mother loves you very much. And it is very important for you to know that, especially now. But she isn't as adept with words as you are and might have a hard time telling you so sometimes."

Cornelia still said nothing.

"One of the reasons you and I got along so beautifully from the very start is because we both love words so much," Virginia continued. "We both wend in and out of dictionaries and tales and books, and so we understood each other very well right away."

Cornelia blinked back a tear. "But my mother doesn't understand or speak that language," she said. "Except for last night, she hardly ever talks to me at all. And I already *told* you that she doesn't even care about words and stories like we do."

Virginia leaned toward the silver tray and poured herself a cup of tea.

"Did it ever occur to you that your mother speaks through music and not words? And that is a very complicated, nuanced language indeed. Every note on every sheet of music is a word on a page to her. Every note she plays on her piano is a word spoken. If you want her to try to understand your language, you're going to have to start trying to understand hers as well. I don't mean that you have to become a pianist like her. I know your reasons for avoiding that path. But you *must* try to live in her world more than you do now."

Cornelia must have looked defeated, because Virginia added, "And that is not a dreary assignment, by the way. If you grow to understand both music and words, there will be no stopping you in this world."

She watched Cornelia for a second. "When I first met you, many months ago, you were such a closed book, Cornelia," she said. "You wove yourself into a maze of longer and longer words so nobody could find you. And now you use words as bread crumbs through that maze. When I first met you, you used dictionaries as fortresses. Now you're beginning to understand that the words in those heavy books are also about the stories those words compose. And, like I've always told you, stories exist to be retold and shared with others.

"Not that I'm not impressed that you know such long words," Virginia continued. "But sometimes I think that the simplest language is the best language. Listen to this."

She pulled an old book out from under the sheets. Cornelia could not see its cover.

"This is a conversation that takes place between two

friends," Virginia explained. "One friend has just saved the other's life. And the one who saved the other one is telling him why she helped him in the first place." She began to read:

> "'Why did you do all this for me?' [the first friend asked]. 'I don't deserve it. I've never done anything for you.'
>
> "'You have been my friend,' replied [the second friend]. 'That in itself is a tremendous thing. I wove my webs for you because I liked you. After all, what's a life, anyway? We're born, we live a little while, we die. . . . By helping you, perhaps I was trying to lift up my life a trifle. Heaven knows anyone's life can stand a little of that.'"

Cornelia listened attentively. "I've heard that before," she said. "What is it?"

Virginia clapped the book shut. "It is from *Charlotte's Web* by a wonderful writer named E. B. White. You probably read it when you were younger. It is a children's book—but the simple words in it say more than most grown-ups can say with every long word in the dictionary. Don't you agree?"

Cornelia did agree. Her heart filled with love for her friend, and at the same time, she was sure that it was going to break.

"Virginia," she said softly.

"Yes?"

Cornelia swallowed. "Are you afraid of dying?"

For the first time in their friendship, Virginia's eyes filled with tears.

"A little bit, Cornelia." She took a deep breath. "But you have to remember that I have done a lot of living in my seven and a half decades. And Alexandra, Beatrice, and Gladys have been gone for many years now. I miss them with all of my heart. Maybe I'll meet them again when I leave this world, and we'll have the biggest adventure of all." She was quiet for a moment. "You just never know what's going to happen."

Just at that moment, the record finished playing and the old phonograph clicked off. Yet they could still hear the soft sound of Mozart playing. After a minute, Cornelia realized that it was Lucy playing the piano in the apartment next door.

For a long time, the two friends sipped tea and quietly listened to the faint music together through the sky-colored wall of Virginia's Indian bedroom.

Epilogue

"You must be very pleased that school's out for the summer," the saleswoman said to Cornelia. "Although New York City gets so hot in July," she added complainingly.

"Yes," answered Cornelia. "But my mother is taking me away on a vacation with her. To France. That's why I need these new suitcases."

The saleswoman looked over Cornelia's new luggage, brown leather with gold letters all over them. Cornelia liked the bags because they looked so old-fashioned, and reminded her of one of the books in Virginia's English library.

"Well, I do admire your choice," the saleswoman said, tapping away at the register.

"She inherited her mother's good taste," Lucy said, paying for the suitcases. "Let's go home and have some lunch, darling," she said to Cornelia.

Cornelia looked out the window of the taxi as they drove downtown. They sped past Central Park with its zoo and tall green trees and sailboat pond. Down Fifth Avenue with its famous hotels and fancy stores. Past the dirty electric shock of Times Square, past the train station, and finally into the confusing tangle of streets in Greenwich Village. Cornelia could see the Hudson River gleaming as they neared her building.

Walter helped Lucy and Cornelia heave the suitcases out of the taxi's trunk and into the elevator. Cornelia lowered her head as they walked past Virginia's front door to their own apartment. There was a pale square above the doorknob where the blue ATTENTION! CHIEN BIZARRE sign had been.

Virginia had been gone for several months now. Recently, two tall women with immovable blond hair had gone into her apartment with clipboards, and a few days later, all of the furniture had been carted away to auction. Out went the grand desk from the library, the Moroccan daybed, the fountain, the Saraswati statue, Cornelia's white chair—even the twenty palm trees, roots and all. Then workers had gone into Virginia's beautiful apartment and chipped away the marble tiles in the Moroccan room and the cloister of the Indian room. Dusty bins lined the hallways as workers filled them with broken tiles and wood. And after that, they set to work making the apartment look just like Cornelia's again, with its stark white walls and wood floors. Just like it did before Virginia and Patel had arrived.

A new young couple moved in when the workers were done. The couple had a baby, and the little family was very quiet. Every time Cornelia thought about the smashed, vanished kingdom next door, her throat tightened.

Madame Desjardins opened the front door the second Lucy put her key into the lock.

"Oh!" said Lucy, surprised. "Thank you, Dominique. Can you help us with Cornelia's luggage set?" She tugged a trunk through the door.

Madame Desjardins had a strange look on her face. "Cornelia Street has a guest," she said.

"Is it Natalie?" Cornelia asked hopefully. She wanted to say good-bye to her friend before she and Lucy left on their trip the next day.

"No," said Madame Desjardins. Lucy and Cornelia looked up at her. "The guest has asked to speak with Madame Lucille first, and is waiting in the study. With a package for Cornelia."

Lucy raised her eyebrows at her daughter. "Wait here, darling," she said, smoothing down her hair. She walked down the hallway, entered the study, and closed the door behind her.

Cornelia was wild with curiosity, but of course, Madame Desjardins wouldn't let her eavesdrop at the door. So instead Cornelia anxiously paced all over the apartment: through the kitchen, the living room, all of the bedrooms upstairs, and back again. As a last resort, she grabbed the cup from the upstairs bathroom and ran down into the piano room. While Madame Desjardins busied herself in the kitchen, Cornelia held the cup against the music room's red wall and pressed her ear to the cup's bottom, trying to catch snippets of the conversation taking place in the study on the other side.

"Cornelia Street!" said a voice behind her. It was Lucy, standing in the doorway of the piano room. Cornelia leaped about five feet in the air. "What do you think you are doing?"

"Nothing," said Cornelia guiltily, and skulked away from the wall.

"Go ahead into the study, darling," said Lucy, gesturing to her. "I'll have Madame Desjardins bring in some tea for you."

"Who is it?" asked Cornelia as she ran into the hallway. Her heart pounded nervously as she opened the study door. When she opened it, she could hardly believe her eyes.

Sitting there neatly on a couch inside was Patel.

"Hello, Cornelia-ji," he said, standing up.

Cornelia ran into the room and threw her arms around him, tears flowing down her cheeks. She hadn't seen him since Virginia died months ago. She didn't let

go for a long time, and he patted her hair while she hugged him.

"Hello, Patel-ji," she managed finally.

"I have missed you," he said, sitting down again. "And so has someone else." He pointed under the desk.

"Mister Kinyatta!" Cornelia shrieked, and dove on her stomach down onto the floor next to the sleeping dog. He woke up and blinked sleepily at her, and gave her hand a few lazy licks. Cornelia kissed the dog on the forehead and felt the little pads of his feet. She was still crying and tried to collect herself.

"I have come to bring you some presents, and then say good-bye," said Patel. "Come sit down, Cornelia-ji."

Cornelia scrambled over to the couch and sat very close to him. It was so strange to see him in *her* apartment for a change, after all of Cornelia's visits to the world next door.

"Where are you going?" she asked, drying her eyes.

"I am going back to India," he answered. "Although to me, home was always where Virginia-ji was. Now I will have to make my own home. So I am starting at the very beginning again."

"I miss Virginia," said Cornelia. "I miss her stories and I think about her all the time."

"Yes," said Patel. "I miss Virginia's stories very much as well. You never knew where her true memories ended and her imagination began. But that never really

mattered, did it?" He smiled sadly. "Virginia-ji has left you something." He held out a package wrapped in brown paper.

Cornelia took it from him and held it in her lap. Her heart beat faster and she felt a bit light-headed. She edged her fingers under the brown paper and tore it away. There was a book inside. Cornelia turned it over to read the title. The front cover of the book proclaimed:

Cornelia looked at Patel in astonishment.

"There is also an inscription inside," he told her. She opened the book and saw a note in Virginia's handwriting:

Dear Cornelia S.,

Just to tide you over until you start having adventures of your own. The torch has been handed

over, and you are officially the new Scheherazade of Greenwich Street. Forge onward and upward.

Your friend always,

V. S.

Cornelia turned the book from side to side. "What *is* this?"

"It is Virginia-ji's last book," Patel explained gently. "About you."

Cornelia was speechless. She opened it up. There were eleven chapters, and at the beginning of each one was a bright illustration, depicting Cornelia, Lucy, Alexandra, Beatrice, Gladys, Patel, Mister Kinyatta, and, of course, Virginia herself. Something suddenly dawned on Cornelia.

"Patel—are these your paintings?" she asked, looking at the pictures in the book. "Is this what you were working on all the time when I came over?"

"Yes," Patel admitted. "Virginia-ji and I were working on this for many weeks. We tried hard to keep it a secret from you.

"There was something about you that inspired us," he continued. "You made us think about many wonderful things that happened years ago. Virginia loved you, Cornelia-ji. You reminded her that life continues in a cycle, and that she still had many gifts to give before she died."

Cornelia sat quietly on the edge of the couch, hugging the book to her chest. "I don't want you to leave, Patel," she said.

"When you are older, you can come and visit me in India," he said. "And in the meantime, you can send me letters about what you are doing. And of course, you must give me news about how Mister Kinyatta is doing as well."

"What?" said Cornelia, looking down at the small dog in surprise.

"I cannot bring him with me," said Patel. "Your mother says that he can live here with you now. Anyway, he does not like me. Besides Virginia, you are the only one Mister Kinyatta does not like to bite. I know that you will take good care of him. Maybe you can take him to buy little cakes, like the first day you met him."

Cornelia put her head on Patel's shoulder and tears dampened her cheeks again. "Thank you," she said, her heart filled with happiness and sadness at the same time. "If Mister Kinyatta ever has a puppy, I'll name him Mister Patel," she promised.

Patel laughed and got up. "It is time for good-bye, Cornelia-ji," he said, and held his arms out to hug her again. Cornelia put her arms around him and squeezed tightly.

Then she watched him leave through the study door and heard him say a gracious good-bye to Lucy. The front door closed behind him, and the last remnant of Virginia's world next door was gone—except for the book that Cornelia held in her hands, and the dog sleeping under the desk.

She picked up Mister Kinyatta and carried him and the book up to her bedroom. There she threw herself into her armchair and began to read. Mister Kinyatta curled up at the foot of the chair and resumed his nap.

A few hours later, Lucy knocked at the bedroom door. "Cornelia," she said. "Can I come in?" She walked in and snapped on the desk lamp. "Mister Kinyatta needs to go outside," she said. "Should we take him for a walk before it gets dark?"

Cornelia clapped her book closed. "Yes," she said. "Let's take the orgulous bezonian out."

"Orgulous" meant "showy and proud," while "bezonian" meant "rascal."

Cornelia followed Lucy downstairs, snapped on Mister Kinyatta's leash, and the family of three walked out onto summertime Greenwich Street.

Acknowledgments

I am extraordinarily grateful to many people for helping me with *Cornelia*—whoever said that writing is a solitary profession? Since I began this project, my life has been bursting at the seams with lavish personalities. And I would like to pass on my adorations to all of them:

First, I am deeply indebted to my wonderful editor, Erin Clarke at Knopf, and my superb agent, Christine Earle at ICM. I couldn't be luckier that *Cornelia* found her way into their hands, these two *grandes dames* in training. Ladies, may our triumvirate set a new standard in the world of neoclassical middle-grade fiction.

And of course, where would I *ever* be without the support and encouragement of Jeff Berg and, in turn, Jim Brooks? I am exceedingly beholden to both of them (like everyone else in Los Angeles and New York, I suspect). Gentlemen, I cannot thank you enough, and for the record, I promise to show up at dinner next time.

Obviously, I would like to thank my mother, Franny, for her unwavering encouragement and vicious edits . . . oh, and for being a glorious pianist and basically inspiring the entire plot of this book. Mom, *merci beaucoup* for allowing me to exploit your entire career and social coterie as material for *Cornelia.* I warn you: this isn't the end, for I know there's a *lot* left to pilfer.

Now I need to turn my attention to Miss Caitlin Crounse, whose devotion and contributions to this book have been on a par with my own. Her beautiful insights about the characters and nature of children's literature provided me with invaluable inspiration at every stage. I couldn't have asked for a more magnificent creative cohort.

I am grateful to Gregory Richard Macek, my very own *bête noire,* for being a stalwart of support, adulation, and foolery throughout this process and so much longer. I'd also like to thank him for his first-time reaction to the eleventh chapter, which nearly broke my heart.

And very importantly, I am much obliged to Miss Sarah Lyon and her mother, Jenny Sour, for their insights into the social world of bookish eleven-year-olds, therefore making plausible to children what is otherwise a work about the lives of sophisticated adults. My thanks also to Sara Just for introducing me to these ladies in what was probably the most unusual booking job she'd done in a long time.

Finally, on a quiet, solemn note, I would like to thank Daisy, whose bohemian vitality and precipitous departure first inspired the idea for *Cornelia*. She will long be remembered with wistful affection by those she left behind.